"Wh

She was not about to exchange pleasantries *and* she refused to give in to the weakening sensations beginning to spread through her body.

He was standing much, much too close to her. She could smell the cold crisp scent of the night on his skin and clothes. If she touched his face it would feel cool, the bones hard beneath his skin, and if he touched *her*...

She swallowed nervously, her eyes darkening betrayingly as they mirrored her confusion and apprehension.

"Now *that* might be construed as a very leading question, or an extremely naive one. Only I don't think naïveté is quite your style any more, is it?"

PENNY JORDAN was constantly in trouble in school because of her inability to stop daydreaming—especially during French lessons. In her teens, she was an avid romance reader, although it didn't occur to her to try writing one herself until she was older. "My first half-dozen attempts ended up ingloriously," she remembers, "but I persevered, and one manuscript was finished." She plucked up the courage to send it to a publisher, convinced her book would be rejected. It wasn't, and the rest is history! Penny is married and lives in Cheshire.

Penny Jordan's striking mainstream novel *Power Play* quickly became a *New York Times* bestseller. She followed that success with *Silver*, a story of ambition, passion and intrigue and *The Hidden Years*, a novel that lays bare the choices all women face in their search for love. Three extraordinary people are fueled by a powerful passion to defy the past in Penny's latest blockbuster, *Lingering Shadows*.

Books by Penny Jordan

HARLEQUIN PRESENTS PLUS
1575—A CURE FOR LOVE

HARLEQUIN PRESENTS
1508—A FORBIDDEN LOVING
1529—A TIME TO DREAM
1544—DANGEROUS INTERLOPER
1552—SECOND-BEST HUSBAND

PENNY JORDAN

STRANGER FROM THE PAST

Harlequin Books

TORONTO • NEW YORK • LONDON
AMSTERDAM • PARIS • SYDNEY • HAMBURG
STOCKHOLM • ATHENS • TOKYO • MILAN
MADRID • WARSAW • BUDAPEST • AUCKLAND

ISBN 0-373-11599-7

STRANGER FROM THE PAST

Copyright © 1991 by Penny Jordan.

This edition published by arrangement with Harlequin Enterprises B. V.

® and TM are trademarks of the publisher. Trademarks indicated with ® are registered in the United States Patent and Trademark Office, the Canadian Trade Marks Office and in other countries.

Printed in U.S.A.

CHAPTER ONE

OF COURSE, it would have to be raining, Sybilla reflected with disgust as she emerged from the supermarket with her overladen trolley.

It didn't help to improve her mood either, she knew, acknowledging that the rain had been forecast and that because she had already been running late she had decided to take a chance and hope that it held off until she had completed her shopping.

The way her life was going at the moment she really ought to have known better, she admitted ruefully as she stood under the shelter of the supermarket building and eyed the vast packed car park.

Her car was parked right at the back; the car park had been full when she'd arrived and that had been the only spot she could find.

She eyed the pencil-slim cream length of her skirt with a sinking heart as she acknowledged how inappropriate a garment it was in which to push a heavily laden trolley across a car park which seemed specifically designed not to ease the transportation of one's shopping to one's car, but to actively hinder it. The rain was becoming heavier; there were puddles on the tarmac, she was wearing a long-sleeved silk shirt, her skirt, brand-new expensive tights and equally brand-new and expensive high-heeled shoes.

She looked, she admitted as she glanced around, rather ludicrously inappropriately dressed for her task.

The majority of the other women shoppers were wearing comfortable, brightly coloured, weatherproof casual clothes, and flat or low-heeled shoes.

But then it was hardly her fault that her business partner's husband should have been involved in a car accident, necessitating Belinda's rushing off to his bedside, while it fell to her to step into Belinda's shoes, give up her precious day off, and take over Belinda's appointments for the day.

Fortunately Tom, Belinda's husband, had not been badly hurt; even so, Sybilla could well understand her friend's desire to be with him.

Perhaps if she hadn't offered to do her neighbours' shopping for them as well as her own she could have put off this trip to the supermarket, but Mr and Mrs Simmonds were elderly and had been so grateful for her offer of help with their shopping that she had felt she couldn't possibly cancel the trip.

Another wry glance at the dense cloud-packed sky confirmed that the rain wasn't likely to let up, and, since she could hardly stay where she was for the rest of the day, nor somehow magic her car to miraculously appear at the supermarket door, she really had no alternative but to accept that she was going to have to get wet and minimise the damage to her clothes as best she could.

Gritting her teeth, she stepped out from under the canopy, resolutely pushing the trolley in front of her, groaning when she discovered that she had somehow or other managed to find herself one of those rogue trolleys with four wheels that appeared to want to go in the completely opposite direction to that she was pushing in.

It was too wet and she was too impractically dressed to get down and try to free the jammed wheels, which meant that somehow or other she was going to have to control the trolley by leaning against the left-hand side of it at the same time as she pushed it.

Normally blessed with a good sense of humour, Sybilla reflected that today was most definitely not going to be her day.

She tried not to imagine what the muddy spray of water from the tarmac was doing to the backs of her legs, and was within a few yards of her car, and just about to give a soft sigh of relief, when a large expensive-looking Daimler saloon car swept towards her.

Automatically she stopped, trying to pull the trolley out of the way, but, instead of it responding to her wishes, the inadvertently sharp tug she had given it made it yaw dangerously to one side.

Of course, she made an immediate grab for it, but it was too late; dangerously overladen with the burden of her neighbours' shopping as well as her own, to her absolute horror the trolley started to tip to one side.

As she leaned across it to try and steady the trolley it bumped painfully into her shin, and she felt the metal tear into the fragile fabric of her tights before finally toppling over.

The car, meanwhile, which had been the unwitting cause of her downfall, had stopped a couple of yards away, the driver no doubt intending to reverse into the empty parking space nearby.

Naturally enough, though, Sybilla didn't have much time to spare to pay attention to what was going on around her. She was far too concerned about how she was going to get her trolley back on its wheels, so at first she did not pay any attention to the opening and closing of the car door, save to mentally acknowledge that it had occurred with a very soft and expensive clunk, rather than with the sharp tinny sound her car door made.

To be confronted therefore with a pair of immaculately polished male shoes, topped by equally immaculate and very expensive-looking dark-coloured trousers, startled her so much that she automatically abandoned the trolley and tried to stand up, horribly conscious of the appearance she must present: her fair hair hanging in rain-sodden strands around her face, her cream shirt and skirt no doubt liberally spattered with dirty rainwater-spots, her tights ripped beyond redemption, and her general appearance was one of a woman so totally unable to control her life that she was not in the least surprised that the man seemed to assume that she needed some help.

She would have accepted it, and thanked him for having the consideration to offer it, if, just as she was getting to her feet, she hadn't heard his voice.

Immediately she froze, recognising it instantly, even though she knew it must be all of a decade since she had last heard it. True, in that decade it had altered, deepened, hardened perhaps... certainly matured, but there was no evidence that his years of working in America had altered his speech pattern. As the man put out his hand to help her to her feet Sybilla withdrew icily from him and, without bothering to lift her head and look at him, was just starting to say coldly and admittedly untruthfully that she could manage when the passenger-door of the Daimler opened, and a woman wearing a pair of high-

heeled shoes even more expensive and less
weatherproof than her own came clicking across
the tarmac towards them, exclaiming in a bored
voice, 'Gareth, what on earth is going on? We're
going to be dreadfully late, although why on
earth you couldn't have got your grandfather's
solicitor to come up to the house instead of our
having to trail down here into this dreary little
town...'

The sharp, petulant words suddenly ceased.
Deliberately refusing to look at or acknowledge
either of them from her semi-squatting position,
Sybilla turned her back on them and then started
to get to her feet.

Behind her she could hear the woman saying
contemptuously, 'For goodness' sake, Gareth,
let's go. What an idiotic thing to do. Stupid
woman.'

Sybilla could feel the hot angry colour rising up
under her skin. She had always cursed its fair-
ness, just as she had always hated her soft fair
hair, longing for the more dramatic colouring she
so envied in others: thick, curly, almost black
hair, warm olive-tinted skin that tanned quickly
and, well, eyes that were a sharp definite colour
rather than softly luminous and somewhere between lavender and grey.

In the old days Gareth had always favoured
girls with exotic semi-Mediterranean looks. She
remembered one whom he had brought home

from London with him, a dark gypsy-like wildness about her, a full, pouting red mouth, sparkling brown eyes... She and Gareth had been inseparable. She remembered how she had envied her... resented her. She had been fifteen at the time, Gareth almost twenty-two.

She suppressed the small stab of remembered pain. She had been such a child, nursing a huge crush on someone so unobtainable that her silly childish love for him had been totally ludicrous.

She had heard him say so himself. Not to her, of course. No, the conversation she had overheard had been between Gareth and his grandfather.

She had gone up to the house on the pretext of visiting Gareth's grandfather, but in reality hoping for a glimpse of Gareth, and perhaps, just perhaps he might deign to spend a few heavenly minutes with her, talking with her.

She had used the side-gate to the garden, scrambling through the undergrowth, pausing as she'd reached the summer house and heard Gareth's voice.

What had prompted their conversation she never knew. All she did know was that, as she'd frozen outside the summer house, hearing with awful clarity every single word of what was being said, in that handful of seconds her childish adoration for Gareth had changed into a corrosive and bitter self-contempt, a loathing of her own immaturity, her foolishness, so that in that moment it was as though she had been split in two, one half of her still being the foolish child who had so stupidly worshipped Gareth, the other a new Sybilla, an adult, aware Sybilla, who could see her folly for all that it was.

Yes, of course—he had eyes in his head, Gareth had said. Of course he could see how Sybilla felt about him. Of course he was aware of the dangers of the situation, and of course he intended to do all that he could to remedy it. It would make his task easier, he had pointed out grimly to his grandfather, if he had not encouraged Sybilla to treat the Cedars as though it were her second home.

'I like the lass,' Thomas Seymour had replied gruffly, warming Sybilla's chilled heart. 'She's got a kind heart, bless her. This place is like a morgue when you aren't here, Gareth.'

'Well, you know the remedy for that, don't you? Sell it and buy something smaller. Move closer to town.'

Sybilla had crept away while they were still arguing.

She knew all about Gareth's desire for his grandfather to sell the large house where he lived virtually alone and to move to something smaller and more convenient; but Thomas Seymour was as stubborn as his grandson. The Cedars had been in the Seymour family since the first

Seymour had set up business in the town during Queen Victoria's reign.

That business still existed, and Thomas Seymour had continued to run it right up until his death three weeks ago.

Sybilla knew that Gareth was back, of course. She could not have failed to do so. Everyone knew. What no one knew as yet was what Gareth intended to do with the business he had inherited from his grandfather.

The two men, so close in so many ways, had never been able to work in harness. They had tried it when Gareth left university, but had quarrelled too often and too passionately for it to work. Gareth had gone to America, carving a new and very successful career for himself in the development of the kind of laser technology he had wanted to introduce into the family firm and which his grandfather had steadfastly refused to allow.

As a result of Thomas Seymour's refusal to move with the times the Seymour business had over the last decade slowly fallen into a decline. The rumours in the town were that, now that Thomas was dead and Gareth had inherited, he would find a buyer for the business or close it down altogether.

Sybilla had refused to be drawn into any kind of verbal speculation about what Gareth might or might not do. She told those who commented on it that she really had no interest in either the business or Gareth himself, her voice losing a little of its normal husky thread of amusement and becoming instead cool and just a little withdrawn. Her too-fair skin might still betray her on occasions, but she had learned over the years how to skilfully deflect attention from areas that caused her anxiety and discomfort, and unfortunately Gareth Seymour had continued to remain one of those areas.

Of course, she was long over that idiotic crush, but the soreness, the humiliation, the sheer mental angst of discovering that not only did he know how she felt about him, that he was aware of what she had truly believed to be her own secret and very personal feelings, but that he could so callously and cruelly make light of them, still lingered.

That was when she had realised the huge gap that yawned between a girl of fifteen and a man of twenty-two, when she had actually realised the difference between being a child and an adult, when she had realised that in order for her to bridge that gap, in order for her to become an adult herself, she was going to have to become like him: cruel, unfeeling, unkind. And she had known that she was not ready to take such a drastic step, that she preferred to remain as she was, and so she had stopped surreptitiously dabbing on immature touches of make-up, had stopped trying to behave and dress in a way she considered grown-up, and had instead reverted to the safe comfort of adolescence; back to her ancient jeans and old sweatshirts, back to tying up her hair to keep it off her face . . . back to spending her time roaming the countryside about her home instead of poring over fashion magazines and wishing that there was some way she could transform herself into the kind of dark beauty she had known Gareth preferred.

The hair colourant, bought on impulse but not as yet used, had been thrown into the dustbin, the allure of its promise of shining raven locks ignored, the make-up she had bought with her precious earnings from her paper-round pushed to the back of her dressing-table drawer.

If her parents had wondered why, after haunting the Cedars, she never went near the place until she was sure that Gareth had returned to London, they had been too tactful to mention it.

In the intervening decade she had meticulously seen to it, then, on his brief visits home, that they never ran into one another, and she had intended to keep things that way.

However, if fate had decreed that their paths must cross she would have chosen for them to do so under far different circumstances from those occurring right now, with her virtually kneeling at his feet, looking for all the world very much like the ungainly, scruffy fifteen-year-old she had been and not the elegant, assured twenty-five-year-old businesswoman she now was.

No, she decided bitterly, today was most definitely not her day.

She stayed where she was, praying that he wouldn't recognise her, waiting for him to answer his companion's imperious summons and walk away, but to her consternation he stayed right where he was, ignoring the rejection of her tense back, ignoring her determination to pretend that he wasn't there, ignoring, it seemed, everything else and everyone else.

Out of the corner of her eye she saw him right her recalcitrant trolley and then start to pick up her shopping.

Both of them reached for the can of shaving-foam she had bought for her neighbour's husband at the same time, his hand impossibly brown, his fingers hard and warm as just for a second they touched hers.

Once that casual, inadvertent touch would have sent her into transports of teenage delight, would have stirred her as intimately and erotically as a far more personal and passionate touch, and perhaps it was because of that . . . because of her memories . . . her awareness of how vulnerable to him she had once been that she snatched back her hand, curling her fingers closed, not quite able to stifle her small betraying gasp of shocked protest.

Of course, all that did was to have exactly the effect she had feared, making him focus on her and study her, and even with her head averted, and her hair swinging forward to conceal her profile he still managed to recognise her.

'Sybilla. It is you, isn't it?'

What could she say? Undignified and idiotic to continue to try to ignore him.

Instead she had to struggle to her feet and from somewhere find some semblance of a polite contained smile, one that acknowledged his recognition of her and at the same time made it clear that the past was exactly where she wanted to keep her memories of him.

'Gareth, I'd heard you were back.'

'You didn't attend the funeral.'

Was that a hint of criticism in his voice? She swallowed hard, refusing to allow it to jar her conscience. It was true that she had stayed away from Thomas's funeral, and equally true that she had done so simply because she had not wanted to run into Gareth. On the face of it it could seem as though she had simply not cared enough for the old man to pay her last respects, but that had not been true. She had loved him almost as if he had been the grandfather she had never had, had loved him and had respected him, even though in recent years she had become increasingly aware that his once firm grip on his business affairs was slackening...that the company was in fact going downhill.

She had made sure she was out of town on the day of the funeral.

Her father was now retired and he and her mother were living fifty miles away, close to her brother and his family. They had been away on holiday when Thomas died, and she had used their absence as an excuse to pay a duty visit to their home to make sure that everything there was in order and safe from burglars or any other damage—a weak excuse, but it had been the only one she could find, unable to face the thought of confronting Gareth *and* dealing with her grief.

If her friends were surprised by her decision, knowing how close she had been to Thomas towards the end of his life, they were too tactful to make any comment.

His death had come as a surprise to the whole town. It was true that he was well into his eighties, but he had always seemed so strong...so alive.

Privately Sybilla believed that, given the choice, he would have much preferred the immediacy of his fatal heart attack to a long-drawn-out period of illness, but that did not stop it being a shock to all those who had been close to him, herself included.

His only close family had been Gareth, but he had had many friends, and, even though a man-

ager had been appointed to run the business,
Thomas had still put in an appearance at the factory every working day.

His presence would be missed in the town.

'My parents were away and I had promised
them I'd keep a check on their house,' she responded coolly now to Gareth's comment.

She had no alternative but to stand up and
confront him. He was, she noticed, still holding
the can of shaving-foam . . . and he was looking
at it in a very odd and angry way.

She swallowed hard, averting her face, determined not to allow herself to be affected by his
maleness . . . his presence . . . his sheer irritating but
overwhelmingly undeniable masculinity.

'Please don't let me delay you,' she told him in
a controlled frosty little voice.

'You're not,' he responded quietly and, she
suspected, untruthfully. Certainly his elegant female companion seemed to think so, to judge
from the increasingly petulant expression mar-
ring the model-like perfection of her features.

Surprisingly she wasn't a brunette but a
blonde, a rather cold and icy-looking blonde in
Sybilla's opinion, for surely those sharp blue eyes
were a touch too sharp, a touch too hard. Certainly they were assessing her in a very critical and
condemning fashion, subjecting her to surely a
far more intense scrutiny than she actually mer-
ited.

'Gareth, we're going to be late,' she protested a second time as Sybilla firmly turned her back on him and started to gather up the remainder of her purchases.

He was still holding the shaving-foam, and as she stood up, dropping her armful of things into the trolley he, instead of adding it to the pile, handed the can directly to her so that she was obliged to reach out towards him for it.

'Yours, I believe.'

Something about the way he said it made her focus on him.

The grey eyes were regarding her almost remotely, his face a mask she couldn't read. In maturity it had a hard-boned masculinity that made her suddenly sharply aware of him as a man in several ways her innocent teenage self would never have been able to be aware of. Not that she was exactly what one might describe as a woman of the world. Far from it—unlike Gareth's woman friend, to judge from her appearance and demeanour.

There had been boyfriends, of course; dates, parties, the usual round of social entertainments, but for some reason she had never felt comfortable enough with any of the men who had dated her to allow them to get too close to her or too intimate with her, either emotionally or sexually.

She reached out to take the shaving-foam from Gareth, conscious as she did so of a certain mental withdrawal, a discernible coolness in the way he was regarding her.

Well, why should that surprise her? He had always treated her with a certain aloof disdain, even if for a while in her teens she had foolishly managed to persuade herself that there was an imagined degree of warmth, of caring in his manner towards her.

But then, teenage girls were notorious, weren't they, for building their castles of dreams on impossibly insecure foundations?

She couldn't really blame Gareth for deriding her foolish adoration of him, but she was determined never to allow him or anyone else to affect her emotions so dangerously again, and, even more importantly, to make it abundantly clear to him that, however foolish she might have been at fifteen, that foolishness was now safely behind her.

The teenager Sybilla had been had lost no opportunity to be with him, seeking him out on the flimsiest of excuses, haunting the house where he had grown up under the guardianship of his grandfather, hanging adoringly and blushingly on his every word . . . silently begging him to notice her . . . to want her . . . to love her.

But that teenager no longer existed. Firmly from the moment she had overheard and realised that he knew how she felt about him, and that it was the subject of open discussion between himself and his grandfather, she had been determined to show him that he was wrong, that he meant nothing to her, and it was for this reason that she had so strictly adhered to her resolve to ensure that she never came into any kind of contact with him, either by accident or design.

At least no one could ever claim that today's unfortunate accident could be anything other than an unwanted coincidence. Not even Gareth himself.

She took a box of tissues from him, almost snatching at it in her desire to escape from him just as soon as she could. And why on earth the sight of a can of Mr Simmonds' shaving-foam should cause him to glare at her so disapprovingly, she really didn't know.

'Oh, do come on, Gareth.'

The blonde was glowering at her now, making it plain how she regarded her, her hand reaching possessively for Gareth's arm, scarlet nails gleaming dangerously against his suit-clad arm.

'You know you're mentioned in the will?'

Sybilla had almost turned away from him, but his curt, almost acid words stopped her. 'Yes,' she agreed tonelessly, without looking at him. Henry Grieves, Thomas's solicitor, had already been in touch with her about the collection of

Dresden figures, which Thomas had directed were to be hers.

She had been a little girl of no more than six or seven the first time she had seen the figures and fallen in love with them. Now she blinked away emotional tears, trying not to remember how at Christmas Thomas had told her that he had left them to her.

He had always said that eventually the figures were to be hers, but she had treated his comments as a joke, knowing how valuable they were, and knowing also that Thomas knew that her love for them had been formed in the days when she had had no knowledge at all of their financial worth.

In many ways she would have preferred that he had not left them to her, even though she appreciated that they had been a gift of love.

Now though, sensitively suspecting that Gareth was somehow criticising her... perhaps even suggesting that she had pressurised Thomas into leaving her such a valuable gift, she tensed defensively.

'I only mention it because you haven't come to collect the figures.'

His mildness confused her, coming so quickly after his earlier apparent coldness.

She couldn't tell him that the reason she hadn't been up to the house was because she had known he was there.

In the distance a church clock struck the hour, causing Gareth to frown. 'I have to go now, but . . . we really ought . . .'

'Gareth, for goodness' sake . . .'

Sybilla was already turning away from him, determinedly pushing her trolley in the direction of her own car. She was, she discovered, trembling slightly, her legs oddly weak.

She told herself it was the shock of her trolley's overturning, but in her heart of hearts she knew it was more than that. That the reason for her unfamiliar and unwanted weakness lay with the six-feet-odd of lean hardened maleness she had just walked away from.

Shaking because of one inadvertent meeting with Gareth Seymour. Ridiculous. She had stopped being vulnerable to him or any other man when she was fifteen years old. Hadn't she?

CHAPTER TWO

OF COURSE, Sybilla could not now go straight into the office as she had originally planned. She would have to go home and change her clothes, do something about her damp hair, and generally make herself look a bit more like the efficient and well-groomed businesswoman she purported to be, before she went through Belinda's diary and dealt with her workload for the day.

Fortunately, Belinda's first appointment wasn't until lunchtime, according to their shared secretary.

Five years ago, when the two girls had decided to start up an agency providing temporary secretarial services, neither of them had envisaged how successful they were going to be. The town had been very small and parochial in those days, and it had only been with the opening up of a new motorway system and the consequent increase in small businesses establishing themselves in the newly developed business park just outside the town that the whole area had become more prosperous. Now, in addition to having on their books twenty very proficient secretaries, they could also provide clients with a wide range of other staff, including computer-operators and programmers.

Sensibly so far they had concentrated on ploughing back the profits they'd made into the business and on expanding it slowly and carefully, and only the previous week they had been approached by their local newspaper, who were keen to include them in an article they planned to run on successful local enterprises.

One of the drawbacks of running one's own business, as Sybilla had discovered, was that it left little time for social and leisure activities.

She had a good circle of friends, some from her schooldays, others she had made since through the business; at least twice a week she attempted to visit the town's new leisure centre and spend an hour or more in the swimming pool there, but of late she had found that the demands of their growing business meant that she had less and less free time.

Belinda had said ruefully just the other day that her husband and two teenage children were beginning to complain that they never saw her, and had told her friend, 'It's not so bad for me, but you don't seem to have any social life at all these days, and you know what they say about all work and no play...'

Sybilla had laughed, but too many of her friends were beginning to make the same comments to her, and only last week the next-door neighbours, for whom she had done this morning's shopping, had warned her that she was never going to find herself a nice young man and settle down if she wasn't careful.

Because she liked and respected the Simmondses, Sybilla had refrained from telling them that she was quite happy as she was. Perhaps she had an over-jaundiced view of the male sex, but it seemed to her that, even in this day and age, once a woman was married and had children it became incumbent on her to juggle so many demanding roles that Sybilla felt it was small wonder that so many potentially very successful career women found themselves abandoning the unequal struggle of competing successfully with their male colleagues for promotion at the same time as they tried to meet the demands of their husbands and children.

When she fell in love she would feel differently, Belinda had told her when she'd voiced this view to her, agreeing that, without that leavening magic, to an outsider it could seem that it was always the woman who seemed to have the responsibility for making relationships work, for keeping life harmonious and happy.

Sybilla had contented herself with lifting a cynical eyebrow. She knew quite well that to those who thought they knew her she represented something of an enigma. With her close friends she was warm and affectionate; to those who needed her help—like her neighbours, like Thomas Seymour—she gave it generously and happily, but when it came to men, especially those who indicated that they found her attractive and wanted to get to know her better, she was cool and off-putting.

She knew that her friends presumed that this was because she had dedicated herself to her career and that there was no room in her life for a man who might demand too much from her.

But the truth was that she was afraid of allowing herself to become emotionally involved with anyone.

She had seen too many marriages and relationships break up under the kind of strain that her own responsibility to the business would put on her to want to risk the same thing happening to her. The truth was that, for all her outward demeanour, at heart she was still the same idiotically romantic girl she had been at fifteen.

When she loved she wanted it to be completely and without reserve; and she wanted it to be forever.

Logic told her that she was being both naïve and foolish, and that in setting such impossibly high goals for herself she was almost deliberately making it impossible for her to form any kind of

man-to-woman relationship. Instead of lowering
her ideals a little and accepting reality she was
deliberately withholding from herself the pleasure and happiness she might have found by doing so, and all because she was still punishing
herself for being such a fool over Gareth.

She had been fifteen, for heaven's sake. Little
more than a child. All right, so she *had* behaved
embarrassingly and idiotically, but she wasn't the
only girl who had ever had a crush on someone.
All right, so it was unfortunate that Gareth had
realised how she'd felt, but that was no reason for
her to feel that to allow any man to believe she
cared for him was to open herself to humiliation
and hurt.

Mentally she might be twenty-five, she acknowledged wearily as she parked her car in her
drive, but emotionally she was still trapped in the
time-warp of the girl she had been at fifteen. Not
an admission she liked making, even to herself.

Ten years on and she was still afraid of making a fool of herself over another man in the way
she had done over Gareth Seymour.

Perhaps Belinda was right. Perhaps if she actually was to fall in love . . . But in order to allow
herself to fall in love she would need first to feel
secure in her relationship with the man concerned, and before that could happen . . .

She sighed to herself as she got out of her car.
If Belinda were privy to her thoughts no doubt

she would tell her that she was trying to put the cart before the horse, and chide her that one did not allow oneself to fall in love . . . that love was an inescapable force, too powerful to resist.

Her house was one of a small row of traditionally built stone cottages a mile or so outside the town.

She had bought it three years ago when her parents had moved away; it was large enough for her needs but small enough not to overwhelm her, and, best of all, it had a long back garden, with views from the upstairs windows of the surrounding countryside.

Most of her neighbours were retired couples, although in recent months two young married couples had moved into the terrace, both of them working for the new companies springing up in the town.

The neighbours for whom she had been shopping were both in their eighties and very independent. They had two sons and a daughter, and several grown-up grandchildren, but their daughter and her family now lived in Australia, and their sons lived too far away from them to be able to do much more than visit a handful of times a year, so Sybilla had found that she had taken on the role of an 'adopted' granddaughter to her neighbours.

Now, as she headed for her own back door, Emily Simmonds had obviously seen her and came out of her own house, exclaiming, 'Heavens! What on earth has happened to you?'

Sybilla quickly explained her trauma with the shopping trolley, but had to refuse Emily's compensatory offer of a cup of tea, saying that she had to get changed and rush back to her office.

Once she had carried Emily's shopping into her kitchen for her, she hurried back to her own house, hastily unpacking and storing away her own purchases before running upstairs and into her bedroom.

The image thrown back to her by the full-length mirror there confirmed her worst fears about her appearance.

Her hair had dried now, but the rain had destroyed the sleek silkiness of its normal style and it would have to be rewashed, her skirt was spattered with mud-stains and would have to be cleaned, and as for her shirt...the front of it was still slightly damp, and to her chagrin she realised that where the fine fabric was clinging to her body it had become virtually transparent. The bra she was wearing beneath it was silk too, and her face flamed with angry colour as she realised that in all probability the rain had soaked through that as well, and that Gareth must have...

She swallowed hard, telling herself fiercely that she was a fool and worse if she thought for one single moment that Gareth Seymour would have had the slightest interest in looking at her body either clothed or unclothed.

It didn't take her long to change and redo her hair, and within the hour she was parking her car outside the office she and Belinda rented in the centre of the town.

'Sorry about the delay,' she apologised to Meg as she hurried in.

'No problem,' the other girl assured her. 'Oh, and Belinda rang in to say that Tom's fine, and that she'll be back in tomorrow if you want to take your day off then. I've been through her diary for you. She's got a lunch booked for today with Talbot Engineering. Ray Lewis from Talbot Engineering.'

Sybilla's heart sank. Ray Lewis was a very good client, but as a man... From the moment they had met he had made it plain to her that he wanted more than a business relationship with her, but he was a married man, and even if he hadn't been he was not the type to appeal to her. She realised that his personal good looks and smooth charm might have deceived another woman, but to her they were simply a mask he used to conceal his insincerity and sexual greed.

She had met his wife and had instantly felt sorry for her. It was plain that she adored her husband, and equally plain that she was terrified of losing him, as she most probably would do, Sybilla thought cynically.

Ray Lewis was a rich and successful man, and he was the kind of man to whom loyalty...love...the promises he had made in marriage meant nothing. Sooner or later he would start looking around for a woman he could show off...the kind of woman a man of his financial success ought to have as a wife. Until then, no doubt, he would content himself with a series of unimportant little affairs...but one day...

Sybilla's mouth curled in disgust. She had made it as plain to him as she knew how that the only relationship she was interested in having with him was limited strictly to business, but he had refused to take the hint, and because of this she and Belinda had agreed that he would become Belinda's client.

Socially it wasn't always possible for her to avoid him, but she had begun to hope that he had at last taken the hint. The last thing she wanted to do was to have lunch with him, but Meg was saying quickly, 'He's thinking of expanding the company, and he wants us to provide him with extra part-time staff while he gets things off the ground. I know that when he made the appointment he told Belinda that this was the only day he had available as he was involved in negotiations with his bank for the rest of the week.'

It was the kind of business they just could not afford to turn down. She had, Sybilla acknowledged, no real option other than to take Belinda's place over lunch.

The morning was already virtually gone, and as soon as she had gone through the post it was time for her to leave for her lunch appointment.

Belinda had arranged to meet Ray Lewis at a very popular and very expensive restaurant some miles outside the town. It was the kind of place that was favoured by the well-heeled business fraternity during the day, and the local 'in' crowd at night.

Privately Sybilla found the atmosphere rather oppressive and rich; she preferred both a less rarefied atmosphere and a plainer diet, but it was typical of the kind of place Ray Lewis would choose . . . the kind of place designed to impress.

She had changed into a smart navy suit and a fresh silk shirt. Outside it was still raining but this time she was prepared. Her navy pumps and tights wouldn't show the rain-spots, and she was armed with her umbrella just in case she had difficulty in parking outside the restaurant.

'I've no idea what time I'll be back, although I'll try to keep it as short as possible,' she promised Meg.

The other girl laughed and suggested mischievously, 'I could, if you like, telephone you at the restaurant.'

Sybilla groaned. 'No...don't you dare. It's the kind of place where they bring the phone to the table. Horrendous.'

She was a few minutes later arriving at the restaurant than she had planned. The bar was full, but she could see Ray Lewis. He was standing with a group of people and had his back to her.

As she approached him he turned round and, on seeing her, exclaimed loudly, 'Sybilla!'

And then, before she could stop him, he had taken her in his arms and was kissing her on the mouth.

As she froze with anger and rejection he whispered in her ear, 'I knew that sooner or later you'd start to see things my way. You and I——'

'Belinda isn't available. It was too late to cancel and so I'm taking her place,' Sybilla told him curtly. She couldn't create a scene here in this crowded bar, however much she deplored Ray's behaviour. Nor could she take the risk of publicly humiliating him, much as she would have liked to do so, for his wife's sake if not for her own.

As she tried to manoeuvre herself away from him he held on to her, taking a very obvious delight in refusing to let her go.

She could feel both her temper and her embarrassment increasing, but refused to allow him to see it, instead saying coolly, 'I suggest you let me go, Ray. We're being watched, and I don't think you'd want your wife . . .'

She didn't have to continue. He was already releasing her and stepping back from her. He really was a most despicable man, she reflected, refusing to give in to the craven impulse to look quickly around the bar to see who might have witnessed his unpleasant behaviour. She could only hope that none of their other clients had seen it.

'If I'd known I was going to have the pleasure of your company I'd have arranged to take you out to dinner. Somewhere very private and very discreet, if you take my meaning.'

Sybilla most certainly did. She made no attempt to hide her revulsion from him as she told him curtly, 'This is a business lunch, Mr Lewis, nothing more.'

'Hey, come on, what's with the "Mr Lewis"? And as for all that crap about business . . . you and I both know that potentially we've got a lot more than business going for us. I like you, Sybilla. I like you one hell of a lot. You're a very desirable woman. A very successful woman. Some men might find that threatening, but not me. In fact . . .' He was reaching out towards her again, and instinctively she stepped backwards, tensing as she bumped into someone.

As she turned her head to apologise to them she heard Ray adding sickeningly, 'I find it a turn on. I find *you* a turn on.'

And she knew that the person standing behind her had heard him as well.

Trying not to let either her embarrassment or her anger show, she forced a polite smile to her lips and turned round properly to apologise. And then her face froze as she saw that the man she had bumped into was Gareth Seymour.

Her apology died in her throat. The look he was giving her was contemptuously disdainful, the way he withdrew from any further physical contact with her bringing a hot wash of colour to sting her face.

This was the last person she would have wanted to witness Ray's unwanted advances towards her. Twice in one day now she had been humiliated in front of Gareth; twice she had been made to feel a fool in front of him.

At her side, Ray was asking her what she wanted to drink. Automatically she told him mineral water, unable to drag her eyes away from Gareth's face and the cold contempt so plainly portrayed there.

'Oh, come on. You can have something more exciting than that,' Ray was pressing her.

She shook her head. She rarely touched alcohol and never when she was involved both in business discussions and driving, but Ray was one of those men who seemed to think it clever to insist on overruling anyone who refused a drink, and she suspected that in the end she would be forced to give in and let him buy her a drink she didn't want and had no intention of consuming.

'I know this is supposed to be a business lunch, but there's no law that says we can't combine business with pleasure, and you know already how much I'd like to give you pleasure,' Ray was saying suggestively and far too loudly. Certainly loudly enough for Gareth to have heard him, to judge from the look of distaste that crossed his face.

As she started to turn away from him he said curtly to her, 'The owner of the shaving-foam, presumably. I can't say I'm impressed by your choice of . . . friends these days, Sybilla.'

It was outrageous, unforgivable, and totally and completely uncalled for that he should make such a comment to her. They hadn't seen one another for ten years; they were virtually strangers to one another, and he had no right, absolutely no right at all to pass criticism on her regarding matters about which he was completely uninformed and completely wrong!

She was halfway to opening her mouth to tell him so when she realised what she was doing. Quarrelling with Gareth, and in public too, was the last thing she needed. Far better to treat his unfounded and ill-judged condemnation of her with the contempt *he* seemed to think *she* deserved.

Even so, as she turned away from him she couldn't resist saying under her breath, 'Fortunate for me, then, isn't it, that your opinion of me...or my friends doesn't rate very highly in my personal scale of life's vital statistics?' And then, as she caught sight of the woman she had seen with him earlier in the day coming towards them, she added for good measure, 'As it happens, I wasn't too impressed with your friend either. Scarlet nail-polish at nine o'clock in the morning is rather overdoing things a little, isn't it?'

With that she turned back to Ray and said quickly, 'I'm rather hungry and short of time. Do you mind if we go straight into the restaurant?'

Before he could object she started to walk towards the restaurant, praying that Ray would follow her.

Of all the people to have run into. And why, oh, why had she allowed herself to be baited into that extraordinary and totally out-of-character bitchiness about his woman friend? It had been completely unnecessary...completely over the top. The smart thing, the sensible thing to do would have been to quietly ignore his gibe and just walk away from him. Instead of which she had had not just to go running headlong into trouble, but to actually verbally invite it. Even in the white heat of her resentment and anger she had been able to see that Gareth hadn't been too pleased by her attack on his woman friend, and who in his shoes could blame him?

She remembered how overawed and diminished she had felt by the girls he used to bring home, how young and vulnerable she had felt in comparison, and wondered a little grimly if it had been those old memories, memories she ought to have rooted out and destroyed long, long ago, which had been responsible for today's outburst.

Whatever the cause, it was pointless regretting it now. All she could do was to hope that she and Gareth did not come into contact with one another again.

With a bit of luck they shouldn't do so. He, after all, couldn't be staying around for very long. He would doubtless arrange for Thomas's business to be put up for sale or perhaps even closed down, and he would then return to America, and she doubted that anyone in the town would ever see him again. Over the last few years it had been only his love for his grandfather that had brought him back, and now that Thomas was dead...

Despite the fact that Gareth had refused to join the family business, had wanted to make his own way in life, he and Thomas had always remained close. Always after his visits Thomas was full of what he had done...what he had achieved.

Sybilla had nerved herself to listen to Thomas singing his praises because she knew how much he meant to the older man.

After Gareth's parents had been killed in an accident Thomas had brought him up, and there was a very, very strong bond between them.

Once, naïvely, she had asked Thomas if he had not been upset by Gareth's decision to branch out on his own, but wisely Thomas had told her that Gareth must have the right to define and shape his own life, and that to try and keep him within the confines of their small town when he wanted to be elsewhere would be to destroy the bonds between them and would eventually destroy their relationship completely.

She hadn't understood that then, at seventeen, but she did now. She had already heard from those who had been there how grim-faced Gareth had been at the funeral, and how obvious it had been to the onlookers that he was deeply upset by the loss of his grandfather, even though he had kept his emotions under control.

Now she wondered what role his companion played in his life. Over the years Thomas had never talked to her about the women Gareth knew. She knew that Thomas had wanted him to marry... wanted him to have children, but as yet it seemed that he had not found the women with whom he wanted to settle down. Unless...

Gareth's emotions and future were nothing to do with her, she told herself grimly as the waiter pulled out her chair for her. In fact she had no business thinking about Gareth at all ... or admitting him into her mind. By rights she ought to be concentrating on Ray and the new business they hoped to get from him.

That was, after all, why she was here, and the sooner she made that clear to Ray as well as to herself, the better.

Lunch was every bit as difficult as she had envisaged. Several times Ray tried to trick her into accepting a dinner-date with him, but on every occasion she side-stepped the issue, until in the end he was starting to become truculent and angry with her.

Knowing that she was going to have to confront him, Sybilla told him firmly, 'You're a married man, Ray, and even if I were attracted to you that fact alone would mean that as far as I'm concerned there could not be any kind of relationship between us.'

'The old-fashioned sort, are you? Well, marriage isn't what it used to be, Sybilla. In fact, my marriage—well, let's just say——'

'Let's just not say anything,' Sybilla interrupted him firmly. 'We're here to discuss business, Ray, and nothing more. And now I really do have to leave. I've got another appointment this afternoon,' she fibbed, 'and I need to get back to the office first.'

She could tell he wasn't pleased but there was no way she was going to be blackmailed into a relationship with him she did not want. No way at all.

She was still feeling raw and uncomfortable when she neared the office, her discomfort over lunch lying under her skin like an irritating piece of grit, but not so much because of Ray Lewis. No, the cause of her discomfort lay more deeply buried within her psyche than that. It was because of her run-in with Gareth that she felt so at odds with herself, so angry with herself for allowing Gareth to provoke her into that unseemly, almost juvenile, retaliation. To provoke her. She frowned as she worried at the words. Why on earth should Gareth have wanted to provoke her? Surely, like her, the last thing he could want was any kind of communication between them whatsoever?

He had made it plain enough to his grandfather ten years ago how little he'd relished her childish adoration of him.

Had he provoked her or was she looking for excuses for her own behaviour? Was she...? But no. His comment to her had been a definite and deliberate provocation. Stripping the whole affair of all of its emotional camouflage and looking at it calmly and logically, she could see absolutely no reason for Gareth to have made the comment he had unless he had wanted to provoke her. But why? So that he could give vent to his contempt of her. But why should that be necessary?

Unless perhaps he had wanted to underline to her how much he despised her. Was he afraid that she might still harbour that idiotic teenage crush? Her face burned with indignation at the thought. That had been ten years ago. She had changed since then. She was a woman now.

A woman. Was she? She was an adult certainly, but a woman... She tried not to remember the number of times she had backed off from members of his sex, from all the men who had wanted her... desired her... all the men whose sexual advances she had rejected in a flurry of protests and fear.

Fear not of them as men, but of allowing them to get too close to her in case ultimately they hurt her emotionally. As Gareth had hurt her.

But it was ridiculous to remain fixated on something... someone who had played such a relatively small part in her life. Other girls had similar crushes and went on to form other, more mature relationships; why hadn't she?

Was it something to do with the trauma of overhearing him telling his grandfather that he was aware of her feelings and most certainly did not feel flattered by them? Was it because she was too sensitive...too afraid of loving another man who would not want that love? But that hadn't been love she had felt for Gareth. She had been a child. She had been fifteen ... and an immature fifteen at that, but not too immature to understand what the sensations she'd experienced whenever she'd thought about Gareth meant. She shook her head, trying to clear her mind of so many disturbing thoughts, thoughts she had successfully managed to push to the back of her mind in recent years, telling herself that she was simply one of those women more interested in remaining independent and establishing a career than in men.

By the time she walked into the office her head was aching. Meg exclaimed sympathetically over her pale face and strained eyes, offering her an aspirin.

She shook her head, telling her wryly, 'I'm allergic to them. They always make me most vilely sick. No, I'll be OK. It's just a tension headache, that's all.'

'I hope you're right,' Meg told her. 'There's a bug going round that starts off with a headache and then develops as full-blown flu. Half the town seems to be going down with it.'

'Don't tempt fate,' Sybilla pleaded. 'The last thing we need right now is a flu epidemic.'

There had been several calls while she'd been out, and as she attended to these she started signing the letters Meg had prepared in her absence. At four o'clock she had a girl to interview, a possible new addition to their pool of temps, who had trained as a computer-operator prior to the birth of her first baby, but who now wanted to get back to work. They were always on the look-out for reliable staff, and if Ray did ask them to provide him with extra temps while he was expanding his business they would need to take on at least three new girls. Of course, after her lunch-date with him he might decide to place his business elsewhere. If he did, then he did, she decided grimly, half inclined to wish that he would, even though she knew from a business point of view his was a very valuable contract.

At ten to four Belinda rang to confirm that she would be back at the office in the morning.

'How did the lunch with Ray Lewis go?' she asked.

'Not very well,' Sybilla admitted.

'Mm. I'm sorry I had to land you with that one, but I know how good you are at being tactful and diplomatic.'

Tactful and diplomatic. Well she certainly hadn't exhibited those virtues today, Sybilla reflected a couple of hours later as she prepared to leave the office.

The girl she had interviewed had been very promising, and had left agreeing to think over their terms and come back to them.

Now all she had to do was spend the evening going over the paperwork she was taking home with her, and with a bit of luck the next day she would be able to enjoy the day off she had forgone today.

Her garden was crying out for some attention and she had promised herself that this year she would redecorate her spare room. She had also promised her parents she would visit them and spend more than her normal brief weekend with them, and even Belinda had warned her that if she didn't allow herself a proper holiday this year she would be in danger of becoming a workaholic.

Her head was still aching when she got home and the back of her throat felt sore as well.

She told herself that it was all that talking over lunch that was responsible for her sore throat, sternly refusing to admit the possibility that she was succumbing to the virulent strain of flu Meg had told her was sweeping the town.

She couldn't afford to be ill, she told herself grimly half an hour later as she sipped a mug of coffee. And she didn't intend to be, either.

Even so, at eight o'clock, when her headache still hadn't gone away and her sore throat persisted, she found herself giving in to the desire to go upstairs and soak in the luxury of a long hot bath, prior to indulging in an early night.

Wearily she finished her coffee and headed for the stairs.

CHAPTER THREE

THE bath might have eased the tension of the day from Sybilla's muscles, but it had done nothing to alleviate either the pain in her head or her sore throat, she admitted as she climbed out of the steaming scented water and wrapped herself in a large dry towel, frowning as she suddenly heard someone ringing her doorbell.

She paused, hoping that whoever it was might go away, but she had always been one of those people who found it impossible to ignore either a ringing telephone or a doorbell, and whenever she'd tried the anxiety and guilt she'd experienced had been so acute that she had learned it was far easier to give in and to acknowledge their summons no matter how inconvenient it might be.

It would probably only be Emily, her neighbour, anyway, calling round to thank her for getting their shopping this morning and hopeful for a bit of a chat.

She hurried downstairs, her feet still bare, her body damp beneath her towel, apologising as she started to open the door.

'Sorry to take so long, I was just having a bath——'

And then abruptly she fell silent as she realised that it wasn't her next-door neighbour who was standing there.

'Gareth,' she proclaimed weakly. 'What on earth . . .? What are *you* doing here?'

'Thanks for the warm welcome.'

He was over the threshold and standing in the hall beside her before she could stop him, tall, broad-shouldered, filling the small space, making her realise how small and vulnerable she was in comparison. Without her shoes she barely stood much higher than his shoulder.

She felt a rash of gooseflesh break out on her skin, and a reaction burning deep within her body that made her feel a helpless surge of anger and fear.

It wasn't right that he should affect her like this . . . it wasn't fair. She was over him completely and absolutely. Or so she had believed.

How could he stand there like that, challenging her shock at seeing him, when he must know? She shivered suddenly, sending a small shower of water droplets from her damp hair on to her bare shoulders.

She watched as Gareth homed in on her tiny betraying shudder, grey eyes narrowing as he focused on her.

Her mouth felt unbearably dry. She had to fight an overpowering impulse to flick her tongue over her dry lips to moisten them. As though he knew somehow what she was feeling, he looked at her mouth.

'You know, you hardly look a day older than you did at fifteen.'

The flat hard words jolted through her, hurting her.

What was he trying to say? That, to him, she was as sexually unappealing now as she had been then? Well she hardly needed him to tell her that.

The arrogance of the man! Did he really think...? Resolutely ignoring that sharply painful *frisson* of sensation she had experienced earlier, that brief moment of self-awareness when she had realised that, somehow, some part of her was still physically capable of reacting to him, she responded curtly, 'Really? It must be the poor light in here.'

No doubt he was comparing her make-up-less, shiny face to the *soignée* elegance of his woman friend's sophistication. Well she didn't care what he thought of her, she told herself recklessly. He wasn't the only man in the world, and his opinion wasn't important to her any more. He could think what he wished of her.

'What is it you want, Gareth?' she demanded, refusing to give in to the weakening sensations beginning to spread through her body.

He was standing much, much too close to her. She could smell the cold crisp scent of the night on his skin and clothes. If she touched his face it would feel cool, the bones hard beneath his skin, and if *he* touched *her* . . .

She swallowed nervously, her eyes darkening betrayingly as they mirrored her confusion and apprehension.

As she grappled mentally with the appalling unwantedness of what she was feeling, she heard Gareth saying drily, 'Now *that* might be construed as a very leading question, or an extremely naïve one, only I don't think naïveté is quite your style any more, is it?'

She stared at him, unable to comprehend the implications of his soft-voiced words. In another man she might have judged them sexually provocative, but, coming from Gareth . . .

His manner towards her held a mixture of contempt, disdain, and a quality which was almost a controlled anger, and none of that added up to the kind of response to her which might have led to his making a sexually provocative remark.

She looked past him at the closed front door, reflecting grimly that ten years ago she would have given her very soul for this degree of intimacy with him, whereas now . . . whereas now all she wanted him to do was to go and leave her alone. His presence here in her hallway was too

overpowering ... too ... too emotionally dangerous, so much so that she could almost feel the air
between them crackling with hostility and anger.

And yet why on earth should he be hostile
towards her? Surely not because Thomas had left
her the Dresden?

Gareth had never been avaricious. Thomas had
been a wealthy man, but she knew that Gareth
had always insisted on making his own way
through life. When he was at university he had
taken holiday jobs, refusing to allow Thomas to
increase his allowance, determined to stand on his
own two feet.

So why should Gareth be hostile towards her?
From the moment she had overheard that conversation, had realised that he knew of her feelings for him and deplored them, she had avoided
him, refusing to return to the Cedars until she'd
known he wouldn't be there. A year's sabbatical
after he had finished university and then the fact
that he had opted to work in America meant that
in the two years before he had left university and
taken up his post in Boston she had barely seen
him at all, so surely he could hardly still be angry with her because at fifteen she had dared to
fall in love with him? Nor, logically, could his
anger come from a misplaced belief that just because he was spending a few days back in town
she was going to start mooning over him the way
she had done as a teenager. She had surely al-

ready proved to him that she knew quite well that
her feelings were not reciprocated, and that the
last thing she wanted was to open herself up to
any further humiliation and pain.

So why the anger?

'You've turned into quite some woman,
Sybilla.'

Quite some woman. The way he said it wasn't
a compliment. She could almost taste the distaste in his voice, and she was sure she could see
it quite definitely in his eyes.

As always when she felt herself under attack
she responded with the protective flippancy she
had developed over the years to hide her sensi-
tivity and vulnerability, shrugging her shoulders
as she told him lightly, 'So they tell me.'

'"They"?' His mouth curled in a cynical
smile. 'Ten years ago if you'd understood what I
meant, which I doubt, you'd have gone bright red
and been as embarrassed as hell.'

She was so angry that she could barely draw
breath. How dared he allude so casually to the
past ... to her foolishness, the anguish she had
suffered, the anguish she *still* suffered? All right,
so he obviously didn't like her ... thoroughly
disapproved of ... felt anger and contempt towards her, but that was no reason for him to refer to something which he must know had caused
her a great deal of pain.

'Ten years ago I was fifteen,' she reminded him bitterly. 'A child. Now I'm a w—an adult.'

'A woman, were you going to say?' he challenged her. 'Yes, you're certainly that.' He was looking at her almost broodingly, the grey eyes surely darker, more intense, the muscles in his throat oddly taut.

She shivered again and realised that she was getting cold. A sneeze gathered in the back of her nose. She tried to fight it off, demanding again, 'What are you doing here, Gareth?'

She sneezed as she spoke, making a quick grab for a tissue from the box on the hall table and blowing her nose both loudly and defiantly. In her daydreams she might once have imagined impressing Gareth with the way she had changed, matured... with her cool businesslike demeanour, with her carefully chosen businesslike clothes, with her success... but after this morning's episode and now this...

'I came to return this to you,' she heard him saying, and as she looked at him she saw that he was removing a tube of toothpaste from his jacket pocket.

He was dressed casually tonight: dark-coloured trousers, a shirt with a fine green stripe running through its white background, a green cotton jumper with a dark blouson jacket over the top of it.

As she focused on his hand, he carried on, 'You let if behind this morning. At the supermarket.'

She stared uncomprehendingly at the toothpaste. He had come here, overriding his obvious dislike of her, merely to return a tube of toothpaste. Her lips parted. She stared at him in puzzled confusion.

'You haven't missed it?'

'Er—no...I——' she swallowed '—er——' She stopped as she sneezed again.

'You're cold.' He made the words sound almost accusing. 'You shouldn't be standing here like this...'

'If you hadn't rung the doorbell I wouldn't be,' Sybilla returned defensively.

His eyebrows rose. 'No. You seemed to be expecting someone.'

The way he said the word 'someone' made it plain that he meant a male someone...a lover, in fact. Sybilla opened her mouth to tell him that he was wrong and that actually it had been her neighbour she had expected to find on her doorstep, but then some perverse streak within her made her change her mind and shrug dismissively instead. 'And if I was——'

'It's no business of mine,' he finished for her. 'Maybe not, but, from what I know of your parents, they wouldn't be too happy knowing that their daughter is having an affair with a married man, and, so it seems, not even bothering to attempt to conceal what she's doing.'

Sybilla couldn't believe what she was hearing. To say that she was stunned was most definitely understating her feelings.

She could have denied it, of course, could have told him just how wrong he was, but for some perverse reason she did not do so, reminding him almost aggressively, 'I'm an adult, not a child, Gareth. How I choose to live my life is my concern and mine alone.'

'Is it? What about your lover's wife? But then, I suppose to you her feelings simply don't matter.'

That he should have misjudged her so unfairly filled her with anger and resentment, making it impossible for her to speak.

'Nothing to say? How you've changed. According to my grandfather you're the epitome of all that a woman should be. He sung your praises unceasingly, but he didn't really know you, did he, Sybilla? He couldn't have known you. You publicly flaunt your affair with a married man——'

'I've had enough of this,' Sybilla interrupted him furiously. 'For your information——' She stopped. Why on earth should she even try to defend herself to him? Let him believe what he liked!

'Did you really come here to bring back the toothpaste,' she challenged him angrily, 'or was that just an excuse to——?' She stopped, amazed to see the dull burn of colour rise up under his skin. She was right, she realised. She had unwittingly hit on the truth. The return of the toothpaste had simply been an excuse to come here and berate her. But why? Why on earth should it matter to him how she lived her life? 'Well you've had *your* say, made your views quite clear, and now I'd like you to leave.'

'Before your lover arrives.'

Sybilla glared at him, and told him frostily, 'As a matter of fact, I was on my way to bed.'

'So?'

For a moment she didn't understand, and then, when she did, her face went bright red and she stared at him in bitter resentment, striding past him towards the front door, intending to open it and repeat her request to him to leave.

However, as she side-stepped him in the narrow hallway, keeping as much physical distance between them as she could, he moved too, as though to block her path. Furious with him, she stepped back, inadvertently getting her feet tangled in the trailing hem of her towel.

She felt the fabric pull against her breasts, realised what had happened, and made a frantic grab for the towel, clutching it protectively against her breasts at the same moment as Gareth moved towards her.

His eyes had been focused on her face, but disconcertingly his attention was now concentrated on her body, on where the full swell of her breasts was now far too clearly revealed above the edge of her towel.

He took a step nearer to her, and instinctively she reached out one hand to ward him off. There was nowhere for her to go, her back was already against the wall, but the sharp darts of sensation piercing her had nothing to do with fear.

He had no right to make her feel like this, no right at all, she told herself with feverish anxiety as she tried to avoid him.

But it was already too late: his hands were closing on her bare shoulders, his fingers hard and warm.

'Sybilla.' His voice was rough and angry. He said her name almost as though he hated her.

'Gareth . . . no . . .'

It should have been a protest, but even to her own ears it sounded more like a plea.

She shuddered in his arms as she felt the warm rasp of his breath against her ear. 'Damn you, Sybilla,' she heard him curse just before he kissed her. 'Damn you for making me want this.'

Making him want . . . While her thoughts spun dizzily through her head she tried to cling on to reality, to ignore the physical sensations engendered by his touch, his proximity. She couldn't let him kiss her, couldn't let him see how vulnerable to him she still was . . . how . . .

Later she swore to herself that she had only opened her mouth to tell him to let her go . . . that it wasn't her fault that he had mistaken her intent, that it wasn't her fault that he had mistaken her parted lips, her swift indrawn breath for an indication that she'd wanted his kiss; and then, once his mouth was actually on hers, it was too late for denials, for logic, for reason.

She was lost in a sea of sensation, swept back in the mists of time, a girl again, desperately, madly in love with an idol so far out of reach that even to dream of an intimacy such as this made her young innocent body tremble with shocked excitement.

This was the first time she had ever been kissed in anger, in a fury of bitterness and contempt that made the pressure of Gareth's mouth on hers hard and almost painful, just as the heat and weight of his body was like an impenetrable wall past which she could not push to free herself not so much from him, she recognised numbly, but from the vulnerability within herself, a vulnerability that recognised that, no matter how lacking in tenderness, in care, in all the emotions she had naïvely thought necessary before she could ever respond to a man with desire, there was deep within her a spark that was all too dangerously easily kindled by this unexpected, almost savage intimacy.

As she fought down the fiercely responsive surge of the reaction she could feel threatening her she made a taut sound of protest beneath Gareth's mouth, tensing in his arms, trying to force some space between their bodies, forgetting, as she pushed against his chest with her hands, the fragility of her towel, forgetting everything but her need to stop what was happening to her before he realised how immediately and overwhelmingly she was responding to him.

In retaliation to her attempt to break free, instead of releasing her as she wanted, Gareth bit sharply on her bottom lip. The shock of his action drew a sharp cry of pain from her that startled them both into frozen immobility.

She was shaking now, trembling with reaction. She heard Gareth say her name in a dazed, disbelieving way. His tongue touched her lip where he had broken the skin, but immediately she pulled away.

'Sybilla...'

'Let go of me.'

She pulled back again, this time relieved to feel his grip of her slacken, but her relief turned to embarrassment as he stepped away from her and the towel, which had only been held against her body by the pressure of his against it, slipped downwards before she could stop it, revealing her breasts fully to him, her nipples swollen and hard, her normally pale skin flushed with desire.

For a moment neither of them moved, and then, with a small cry of anguish, Sybilla gathered up the towel, her hands trembling as she hugged it against he body.

'Sybilla——'

'Get out,' she told him in a choked voice. She couldn't endure listening to any more insults right now. All she wanted was to be left alone... to forget the extraordinary and humiliating events which had just taken place.

She turned her back on him, her body clenched tight with tension as she waited for him to go. She heard the door open, felt the cold chill of the evening air... felt him pause as though willing her to turn round, but she refused to do so, only allowing her tense muscles to relax once the door had closed behind him and she was sure he had gone.

When she did relax she was trembling so much that she couldn't move. She had to lean against the wall for support while she tried to control the involuntary reaction of her body.

Her whole mouth felt swollen, her bottom lip was sore where he had bitten it, her breasts ached, and there was a sensation low down in her body... an awareness... a need... a conscious memory of how it had felt to have the hard male weight of him pressed against her.

She gave a violent shudder, trying to free herself from the trap yawning in front of her. This wasn't right . . . it was stupid, sick almost, to be forced to confront the fact that she had actually been physically turned on by him, that she had actually wanted . . .

She swallowed, her throat so sore that the action made her wince. She felt peculiarly light-headed, oddly vague, as though she was suddenly incapable of formulating any kind of logical thought.

Sybilla couldn't wholly come to terms with what had happened . . . that he had actually . . .

She swallowed again. She knew that men could react like that to anger, but in Gareth it seemed so out of character, so unexpected . . . so shocking, somehow. She had never imagined . . . never envisaged . . . In her teenage daydreams she had yearned for kisses that were tender . . . innocently, idiotically chaste . . . for caresses based on a childish view of what desire must be. She had never, ever imagined being kissed the way Gareth had just kissed her, and she had certainly never, not even in her adult years, imagined that she would actually respond to that blending of male desire and male anger. Her body tensed again. She made a small keening sound of despair deep in her throat, ignoring the pain it caused.

She still couldn't believe it had happened, that Gareth had walked in here and actually . . .

She shivered. No doubt if challenged he would claim that it was all her fault, that she had been responsible for his lack of control...that it was her apparent provocativeness, her refusal to back down beneath his accusations which had put the fatal spark to the dry kindling of his anger.

Wearily she went upstairs. Her whole body ached now and she was beginning to suffer the aftermath of her physical and emotional shock.

She would never in a thousand years have imagined Gareth accusing her of having an affair with a married man, of being interested enough in whatever she might be doing to be bitterly condemning and contemptuous of her behaviour, never mind to react to it with so much sexual aggression.

Bewildered and confused, she crawled into bed, hugging the bedclothes around her, curling her body into a small protective ball. Her lip was still sore and swollen, and yet when she remembered his kiss it wasn't with the revulsion she knew she ought to feel.

Instead...instead... Her heart bounded with fright as she tried to deny the *frisson* of sensation that ran through her.

This was crazy...impossible. She *couldn't* feel like that...*mustn't* feel like that...dared not allow herself to feel so...so aware, so responsible, so dangerously and wantonly excited by the memory of Gareth's intensity. What would he be like if that intensity was fuelled by desire...by love, and not by contempt and anger?

She had no right to indulge in such curiosity...no right and no sense either if she did. She was treading a path she already knew could lead only to heartache and pain.

Her head felt as though it were stuffed with cotton-wool; thinking was far too much of an effort. All she wanted to do right now was forget the whole thing...to close her eyes and go to sleep and pray that when she woke up again she would discover that the entire incident had been something dreamed up by her imagination and had not in reality happened at all.

She shivered, despite the warmth of her bed. Her throat felt so sore; her head ached unbearably. She remembered again Meg's warnings about the flu virus, but told herself stubbornly that she was most definitely not going to succumb to it; that it was just a cold—just reaction!

CHAPTER FOUR

SYBILLA had to repeat this promise to herself a dozen or more times during the following day. Despite the fact that it was her day off and she had been looking forward to spending some time in her garden, she discovered that she was suffering from a lassitude, a vagueness, that prevented her from doing anything more energetic and profitable than wandering around the garden a few times, telling herself that she really must start pruning and tidying up but then finding that she lacked the resolve to do anything other than distantly notice that there was work to be done.

The trouble was that her mind was far too full of other things ... too busy with other problems.

Gareth ... who would ever have thought ... imagined? She shivered convulsively, her skin burning. What would have happened if, instead of freezing and rejecting him, she had ...?

Aghast at the direction of her own wilful thoughts, she stared fiercely at the forsythia in front of her. It had finished flowering now and was ready for pruning.

If she had any sense she would go back to the house, collect her gardening clothes and pruning knife and get to work. The fresh air would help clear her head, and, if her throat was aching and she felt slightly shivery and achy, then she ought to be concentrating on willing herself to fight off these symptoms instead of allowing herself to become so absorbed, so obsessed with Gareth Seymour and his inexplicable behaviour.

Listlessly she walked back to the house. A good brisk walk or some other form of strenuous exercise was probably what she needed.

A new country-club complex had opened just outside the town in what had originally been a large derelict Victorian mansion. This had now been converted into a small exclusive hotel, with a large extension added to it which contained conference facilities and a swimming-pool complex with its own bar, games-rooms, a gym, indoor squash and tennis courts and several other features.

It had been Belinda who had suggested that they become members, mainly for business reasons: she and her husband were both keen golfers and used the course attached to the complex, while Sybilla preferred to make use of the tennis courts and swimming pool.

She could drive over there, swim, have a light lunch, and with a bit of luck find that the exercise had restored her normal energy, but instead of going through with this plan she found her mind wandering dangerously and rebelliously in the direction of Gareth.

The woman who had been with him had been extremely glamorous, and yet Sybilla knew instinctively that, despite the fact that his grandfather had wanted him to get married and have children, Thomas would not have taken to her.

Why *hadn't* Gareth married? she mused. She knew how hard he had worked to establish himself in America and how successful he had been. Perhaps that had meant that he had never had the opportunity to form a deep and committed relationship, or perhaps he had just not wanted the tie of that kind of commitment, or just not found the right person. His companion, the blonde... was *she* the right one?

The pain that knifed through her was so sharp, so acutely physical that it caused her arm to shake. Coffee slopped from her mug on to the table. She put down the mug, shocked by her own reaction, fiercely glad that there was no one else there to witness it.

Why, after all these years, was she reacting like this? Gareth meant nothing to her. She had got over that silly adolescent infatuation years ago.

Had she? If that was true, why had she felt such a physical awareness of him last night...why was she thinking about him now, why was she...?

She got up, pacing the kitchen impatiently. This was silly... and, worse, it was dangerous. Thank goodness Gareth would soon be gone and she could get back to normal, forget him, or at least push him to a dusty dark cupboard at the back of her mind and lock it securely, keeping him there.

Now, after all this time had elapsed, the last thing she wanted to do was let herself turn into a victim of her own emotions, trapped by the past, unable to let go of its pain, unable to learn from it and walk free into maturity.

So she had had a mammoth crush on Gareth, and he had known about it . . . had known about it and been angered by it. She wasn't the only teenager in the world to have gone through such an experience.

All right, so it had made her cautious, over-cautious, in fact, in her reactions to other men, but, given the new social awareness of the risk of promiscuity, hadn't that perhaps been a good thing?

Not if it meant that she was so mortally afraid of loving a man who would reject her as Gareth had rejected her that she would not allow any man to get close enough to form any kind of re-lationship with her, she told herself grimly.

The remedy to that lay within her own psyche and was not something she could blame on Gareth. She already knew that.

Yes, she *knew* it, she agreed with herself restlessly, but somehow seeing him ... having him here in her home had resurrected so many painful memories she had thought she had long ago overcome that she felt confused, frightened almost, unable to trust her own mind to guide her logically and safely through the minefield of her own emotions.

When Gareth had kissed her, for one wild, impossible heartbeat of time she had actually wanted to respond to him, to match his anger with her own, his violence, his passion. She touched her sore lip with her tongue, shuddering as she acknowledged that her own anger, her own resentment and bitterness had been such last night that she could have wantonly and willingly inflicted the same kind of physical punishment on him as he had done on her. And that shocked her.

The phone rang and, glad of the distraction, she went to answer it.

It was her mother, ringing to ask if she knew when she was going to be able to visit them. She had to admit that as yet she hadn't been able to work out a timetable with Belinda, but promised to do so just as soon as she could.

It was only half an hour later, when she had replaced the receiver after a long chat, that she realised uncomfortably that she had not told her mother that Gareth was home.

Irritably telling herself that she had wasted enough time for one day trying to untangle the confusion of her emotions, she was just about to force herself to go back outside and tackle the forsythia when the phone rang again.

She reached for the receiver, a tiny tremor of sensation spearing through her when a man's voice spoke her name, but almost instantly she realised that the caller was not, as she had first believed, Gareth, but Ray Lewis.

She felt angry with herself both for that betraying flare of reaction and for being idiotic enough not to recognise Ray Lewis's voice instantly. It was, after all, nothing like Gareth's, being more sharply pitched, more abrasive and yet somehow at the same time less masculine. She responded in an unencouraging clipped voice.

When it transpired that he wanted to persuade her to have dinner with him, under the guise of needing to have further discussions with her about his new staffing needs, her anger got the better of her.

She couldn't forget what Gareth had said to her last night, the assumption he had made about her relationship with Ray Lewis, and now she couldn't help wondering if other people had leapt to the same erroneous conclusions; if others thought that their relationship was not confined to business. If so... if so, no matter how valuable the business he might put their way, that kind of gossip and allusion could only damage the firm's reputation and the professionalism on which Sybilla prided herself.

Because of this she was shorter with Ray Lewis than she had been previously, pointing out to him that he was Belinda's client and that as Belinda was now back in the office his best course of action would be to get in touch with her there.

When he repeated his invitation to have dinner with him she took a deep breath and told him coldly that since he was not her client she could see no reason for accepting his invitation.

When he laughed and said, 'Who said anything about business?' her anger increased. She was, she discovered, gripping the receiver so tightly that the bones in her hand actually hurt. She had no option but to tell him that she was neither interested in nor flattered by what he appeared to be suggesting. He was, she reminded him, a married man, and even if he weren't... She took a deep breath, warning herself that she was over-reacting, that a simple but firm 'No' would probably have been enough, and, to make it worse, she could not honestly say that her over-reaction had nothing to do with Gareth's accusations and assumptions.

She could tell from Ray Lewis's angry and sar-
castic response to her rejection that she had
probably made an enemy of him.

'You're not the only pebble on the beach,' he
told her sneeringly. Then he added, 'I'd be careful I didn't price myself out of the market if I
were you. You're just like all the rest of your sex,
holding out for marriage and a rich husband.
You don't fool me.

'Well I've got news for you. If you really think
that what you've got between your legs is
worth——'

Sybilla replaced the receiver, her stomach
churning sickly with shock and disgust.

She had always known somewhere in the back
of her mind that Ray Lewis was the kind of man
who disliked women and perhaps even secretly
feared them, but this was the first time she had
ever been subjected to that kind of male aggression. It left her feeling dirty...unclean...
frightened and weak in a way that Gareth, for all
his physical exhibition of anger towards her, had
not. Gareth's anger had been clean, untainted by
emotions towards her sex that left her feeling
nauseous and shadowed by unease.

At least she was now sure of one thing: Ray
Lewis would stop pestering her to go out with
him, and if people had been gossiping...had

made ill-founded judgements, they would soon realise they were wrong.

What Belinda would say when she discovered that they were likely to lose his business was another matter. Sighing to herself, Sybilla acknowledged that she could have handled him more tactfully, would probably have handled him more tactfully if it hadn't been for Gareth's accusations.

But why on earth should it matter to her now what Gareth Seymour thought of it? If she had any sense...

But that was just it. At the moment she seemed to be displaying a dangerous lack of that commodity.

Her head was aching again. She was not, most definitely *not* going to give in and allow herself to succumb to this virus, she told herself grimly. She had already allowed herself more than enough self-indulgence for one day, and look how she was suffering for that! No. She was most definitely not going to be ill. Virus or no virus.

She was repeating this mantra to herself the next morning as she dressed for work, fiercely telling herself that all that was wrong with her was a bit of a sore throat and an aching head, and that once she was at her desk and busy she would soon forget the discomfort they were causing her.

Stubbornly resisting the inclination to crawl back into bed and stay there, she went downstairs and had her breakfast.

The sun was out, the sky clear and sharply blue, promising a beautiful spring day, but when she stepped outside there was a cruelly cold wind—or so it seemed to her as she huddled deeper into her jacket and hurried towards her car.

Belinda was already in the office, going through the post. She greeted her with a warm smile which turned to a concerned frown when she heard the huskiness in her voice.

'Are you feeling OK?' she asked anxiously.

'Fine,' Sybilla assured her. 'But I do need to have a word with you. Have you got a minute?'

'Well I've got an appointment at half-past...'

'This will only take a few minutes,' Sybilla assured her. She had been worrying all night about the potential repercussions from her rejection of Ray Lewis, and wanted to warn Belinda that they could well lose his business.

'Let's go into my office,' Belinda suggested.

Sybilla followed her inside, leaving the door half open in her anxiety to tell her what had happened.

'What is it? What's wrong?' Belinda asked her.

'You know the problems I've been having with Ray Lewis?'

When Belinda nodded she continued.

'I saw him while you were off. You know he wanted to discuss taking on more temporary staff?'

'Yes. He discussed it with me. Did he say how many people he would need, and what skills they——?'

'He did, but I don't think we're going to get the business, and it's all my fault, I'm afraid. You see . . . it's . . . it's come to my notice that people, or at least some people, appear to believe that Ray Lewis and I are having an affair and——'

'What? Oh, surely not!' Belinda protested disbelievingly. 'Anyone who knows you. . . . I know he's been making a nuisance of himself——'

'Rather more than a nuisance,' Sybilla interrupted her feelingly. 'When I had lunch with him the other day he virtually tried to blackmail me into sleeping with him. Of course I refused. Even if he weren't married . . . well, let's just say he most definitely isn't my type——'

'Is he anyone's?' Belinda interrupted her drily. 'That poor wife of his—how on earth she puts up with him . . . He has to be one of the most obnoxious men I've ever come across. Every time I have to deal with him I thank my lucky stars that he considers me too ancient and past it to be worthy of his attention. But you didn't mention this when we——'

'No. Because it was only afterwards that I discovered that people were apparently jumping to the wrong conclusion about my supposed relationship with him. And to make matters worse he rang me at home yesterday. When I tackled him and pointed out to him that by rights he was your client he dropped all pretence of wanting to discuss business and...well, to cut a long story short, I had to tell him that he was wasting his time. He wasn't pleased, and I'm afraid it will mean that we will lose his business. I wasn't very tactful, and he... Well, let's just say the way he reacted made me even more determined to give him a wide berth in the future. I'm sorry, Belinda, but I'm very much afraid that we'll lose the account.'

There was a pause, and then Belinda said firmly, 'To hell with the account. I feel very guilty. I had no idea that things had got so bad that he was harassing you like that. I knew he fancied you of course, but you seemed to have things under control, and as long as I dealt with him... But for him to actually threaten you...'

'*I* thought I had it under control as well,' Sybilla admitted, 'but, well, let's just say he's made it plain to me that I don't have, and when it comes to other people gossiping about an affair between us which just does not exist and never could exist...'

All her distaste and horror was revealed in her voice, which shook slightly as Belinda reached out and covered her hand with her own. 'I know how you must feel,' she said softly, 'and I promise you that no one who really knows you would believe for one moment——'

She stopped as Sybilla gave a bitter little laugh.

'What's wrong?' Belinda asked her worriedly. 'What have I said?'

'It's not you,' Sybilla assured her, 'it's——' She stopped as she heard the phone ring in the outer office.

'I'd better go and answer that. Meg isn't in yet.'

As she turned towards the door she almost collided with the man who was just about to rap on it, her face going parchment-pale as she stared at him in shocked dismay.

'Gareth.'

She was hardly aware of having said his name. He was looking at her in such a confusing way. Gone was the anger...the fury of their last meeting, and instead the look in his eyes was one of remorse...of anguish almost.

But that was impossible. She must be imagining things. She blinked slowly and took a deep unsteady breath.

Behind her she heard Belinda saying courteously, 'Mr Seymour, I'm sorry there was no one in the outer office.'

'That's all right,' Gareth was responding, looking beyond her now towards Belinda. 'I'm a little early, anyway.'

'You obviously know my partner.' Belinda looked at her curiously, no doubt wondering what on earth was wrong with her, Sybilla reflected as she virtually bolted through the door, deliberately keeping as great a distance between Gareth and herself as she could.

'Yes, indeed. Sybilla and I are old...friends.'

Friends. They had never been friends, Sybilla reflected bitterly as she retreated to her own office. Oh, she might once have deluded herself into believing that those long hours they had spent together talking had meant as much to Gareth as they had to her, but of course she had been deceiving herself. She had been a girl...a child almost, while he had been a young adult. Even now she writhed in self-mortification to remember the anger in his voice when he had told his grandfather how little he'd wanted her adoration, her hero-worship...how impossible he found it to deal with the situation.

Well, she had made it easy for him, removing herself from his presence, determinedly avoiding him...throwing herself into such an orgy of tennis, swimming and teenage parties that even her parents had started to protest that she was wearing herself out.

Wearing herself out. What she had been trying to do was to wear out her love for Gareth, instead of wearing it on her sleeve.

And she had succeeded too, hadn't she? Hadn't she? Of course. Of course she had.

Why had he come to see Belinda? What possible need could *he* have for their services? she wondered fretfully, unable to settle to her own work, and yet too proud, too stubbornly determined not to show the least bit of interest in him to find an excuse to join them.

A sudden fit of sneezing took her off guard, causing Meg, who had just come into her office with a mug of coffee, to exclaim, 'There, I told you . . . it's that virus!'

'It's no such thing,' Sybilla contradicted her, breaking off to sneeze again, and to curse her own weakness under her breath.

Just at that moment Belinda's office door opened and both she and Gareth walked out. He seemed about to pause, to hesitate as he drew level with her open office door, but she deliberately turned her back on him and started to ask Meg about a file she needed for one of her own interviews later in the day.

It was only when the outer office door had actually closed behind him that she realised how tense she was, and that she was actually physically compressing her muscles as though against some kind of attack. Or some kind of danger.

'Well, there's a bit of luck,' Belinda pronounced as she came back and walked into her office. 'I'd expected that with old Mr Seymour's death the business would be closed down. Everyone seems to have been speculating that that would be the case, but it seems that his grandson is not only going to keep it going but intends to come back here to run it himself.

'He wants us to supply him with half a dozen new key people. Computer experts in the main, who shouldn't be too difficult to find, and a new factory manager, who will...'

Sybilla couldn't say a word. Gareth was coming back and intended to take over the family business, to step into his grandfather's shoes...

She couldn't believe it. She refused to believe it, but how could she when Belinda was talking excitedly about the boost this would give their business, far outweighing what they would lose if Ray Lewis did go elsewhere?

'Not, of course, that there's the slightest comparison between them,' she was saying. 'Ray Lewis is obnoxious, while Gareth Seymour...' She rolled her eyes. 'Now, if I were ten years younger...*and* he's unattached.'

Legally, perhaps. Sybilla wondered how serious his relationship was with his snooty ladyfriend; wondered if he intended not only to step into his grandfather's shoes and revert to family tradition, but also to marry and produce a family...the great-grandchild old Tom had always wanted.

'What is it, Syb? What's wrong? You look dreadful,' Belinda was saying, having at last ceased singing Gareth's praises and realised how white and strained her partner was looking.

'She's going down with the flu bug that everyone's got,' Meg pronounced direfully.

'No, I'm not doing any such thing,' Sybilla almost snapped, and then, seeing their faces, apologised and explained a little untruthfully, 'I'm still a bit on edge after my run-in yesterday with Ray Lewis...and as for being ill...well, I'm afraid I just can't afford to be. It's Rita and Paul Gittings's silver-wedding party this weekend and I can't miss that...'

'Good heavens, no. Paul is your godfather, isn't he?'

'Yes,' Sybilla confirmed. 'And he was marvellous about recommending us when we first set up in business.'

'Yes, he was. I expect your parents will be coming over too.'

'Yes, they'll be there. And Anthony and Claire. They had originally intended to bring the children and stay overnight with me, even though it would have been a bit of a squash, but Simon's in a swimming competition on Sunday, so they'll all be driving straight back.'

While she answered Belinda's questions her brain was seething with anxiety. Gareth moving back...permanently. How was she going to cope with that...with the possibility of seeing him...of knowing that she could virtually bump into him at any time? And then if he did marry...

Her heart gave a painfully sharp leap. Despair filled her. What on earth was the matter with her? She had got over Gareth years ago. He was a stranger to her now. There was absolutely no reason for her to get herself into this kind of state. And what was she frightened of anyway? That he would guess...would think that she was still that same idiotic adolescent who had burdened him with her unwanted adoration, her youthful love? Well, if so, the remedy lay in her own hands. All she had to do was make it clear to him how much she had changed. How indifferent she was to him.

What a pity she wasn't married with a couple of children, she reflected grimly. *That* would have convinced him. As it was, she didn't even have a boyfriend. It was true that there were two or three men in the town who regularly asked her out on dates, but she had always made it plain to them that the occasional date was as far as she wanted any relationship with them to go. Two of them had in fact offered to escort her to the silver wedding, but, since her family would be there, she had kindly but firmly refused. Now she wondered if she had done the right thing.

Of course, it didn't necessarily follow that just because Gareth was going to stay here permanently he would be invited to the party, but the Gittingses had known his grandfather very well, and if he turned up at the party with his *soignée* blonde friend on his arm while she was there on her own . . .

She was being absurdly sensitive, she told herself firmly. She was creating problems for herself that simply did not exist.

She had a busy day in front of her and by rights the only thoughts occupying her mind right now should be confined to the business ahead of her.

The reality, though, was rather different. The reality was that, no matter how hard she tried to concentrate on her work, Gareth Seymour kept intruding on her thoughts, breaking through the barriers she tried to erect against him, so that by six o'clock she felt more physically and mentally drained than she could ever remember feeling, even in the early days when she and Belinda had first gone into business.

'You ought to be in bed,' Belinda scolded her, seeing her wan face when she popped her head round Sybilla's office door to announce that she was on her way home.

'Rubbish—there's nothing wrong with me.' She stopped as Belinda raised her eyebrows, and admitted defensively. 'Well, perhaps I *have* got a bit of a cold, but that's all it is.'

'Says you,' Belinda murmured *sotto voce*, adding more seriously, 'and, if you're still worrying about Ray Lewis, then don't. I've been thinking things over, and quite honestly I believe we're better off without his business; if he's unscrupulous enough to try to blackmail you into sleeping with him then I really think that sooner or later we'd have had other problems with him as well. He's obviously a bully and, like all bullies, he can't resist trying to use what he considers to be his superior strength against those he believes to be weaker than him.'

'Mm...' Sybilla gave a small shudder. '...I suspect you're right, but... well, I honestly believe that he actually hates women. I could hear it in his voice when he rang me. It was quite frightening really. I...'

'I should imagine it was. Look, if he rings you again at home just put the phone down, and if he gets in touch with me—well, I've already decided that I'm going to suggest he takes his business elsewhere.'

'I feel so guilty,' Sybilla told her.

'Well don't. You've nothing to blame yourself for. In fact, I suspect *I* should have realised earlier what a problem he was going to be and done something about it then. You're not staying on here too much longer, are you?'

Sybilla shook her head. 'No. I'm just about to leave.'

She had an interview in the morning with a potential new member of their temporary workforce, a computer-program writer who had apparently moved to the area only recently, and who was presently working sixty miles away in the city, but who wanted to try and find work which involved less travel. While he looked he was apparently prepared to consider working for them as one of their 'temps'. Sybilla was very pleased that he had approached them. They were desperately short of his kind of highly qualified and skilled people; the problem would be not in finding him work but in satisfying the demands of those clients who would want to use his services.

It was almost seven when she finally locked the office door behind her and walked over to her car.

Her throat felt raw and painful and her body was aching, but she was grimly determined not to give in. All she needed was a decent night's sleep and she would feel fine, she told herself firmly as she drove home.

CHAPTER FIVE

SYBILLA'S house was at the end of the small row and therefore had a garage and a short drive. As she turned into this drive she noticed that there was an unfamiliar car parked outside her house. Presumably its owner must be visiting one of her neighbours, she decided uninterestedly.

She frowned a little as she studied its vaguely familiar expensive paintwork.

Wondering who it belonged to, and then dismissing it from her mind as she opened her own car door, she paused while she extracted her house keys from her shoulder-bag.

As she closed her own car door she was vaguely aware of the expensive clunk of another car door closing, but didn't realise who had closed it until she reached her front door and heard Gareth saying from behind her, 'At last! I was beginning to think you were going to work all evening.'

Her response was automatic, instinctive. She turned round immediately, too surprised to conceal her shock, and then wished she hadn't as she

realised how close to him she was. She tried to
take a step back from him and discovered that she
couldn't.

'I have no idea what you want,' she began
tersely, remembering his previous visit, 'but——'

'What I want is to apologise to you.'

The soft words made her gape disbelievingly at
him. 'To apologise...' Without knowing why she
did it, she found that her tongue-tip was
automatically seeking the small wound that still
marked her bottom lip.

'Yes! And for that as well,' he told her in an
oddly rough voice that raised a betraying rash of
gooseflesh on her body. 'But primarily——' He
stopped and raised his hand as though he was
about to touch her.

Immediately she flinched and then flushed
dark red as she realised how betraying and juvenile her reaction had been ... the reaction of a
woman quite obviously not used to a man's touch
no matter how casual or non-sexual.

She tensed, waiting for some sardonic comment, her face averted from him, her fingers
trembling as she tried to insert her key in her
front-door lock and escape from him.

'I suppose I deserved that.' His voice was harsh
again now. 'Sybilla, I'm sorry. I should never...'
He broke off and then said quickly, 'Look, can
we go inside to discuss this?'

Go inside. She opened her mouth to refuse, to tell him that he was the last person she wanted in her home, but before she could speak he was continuing, 'It's just that we do seem to be attracting rather a lot of attention from your neighbours.'

To her consternation, Sybilla saw that he was right. 'Yes. Yes, you'd better come in,' she agreed with obvious reluctance.

So obvious in fact that his mouth twisted wryly. 'Not exactly a warm welcome. But then I hardly deserve...warmth...in the circumstances, do I?'

Why had he hesitated like that over the word 'warmth'? she wondered sensitively. Was he, like her, remembering that once she would have welcomed his presence with a good deal more than mere warmth?

She could feel her face starting to burn again, and because of those memories, because she was so acutely conscious of the past she immediately withdrew from him, physically as well as emotionally, saying in a clipped accent, 'I'm rather tired, Gareth. I don't know what you're doing here.'

'I've already told you: I've come to apologise.'

'What for? Accusing me of having an affair? There was really no need. It's hardly something

of world-shattering importance. After all...your
opinion of me——'

'Oh, I already know you don't give a damn
about my views, my feelings,' he interrupted her,
causing her to pause in the act of removing her
jacket to stare at him.

What she had been about to say was that his
opinion of her had sunk so low when she was a
teenager that it could scarcely have sunk any
lower, and now she was so shaken that it was impossible for her to hide her reaction from him.

She had started to tremble slightly, her fingers
gripping her jacket far too tightly.

'I'm sorry. I'm upsetting you.'

She started to shake her head in defensive denial, and then had to stop as a fit of sneezing
overtook her.

'You're not well.'

He sounded brusque, stern almost, reminding
her momentarily of the time when he had treated
her with a mixture of vaguely older-brotherly
concern mixed with affection and humour.

But those days were gone, she reminded herself fiercely, and that heady blending of affection and humour had never really existed other
than in her imagination. If it had...

She took a deep breath. 'I've got a bit of a
cold, that's all.'

'You shouldn't be standing here in a draught.'

Before she could stop him he was walking her towards her open kitchen door. She had no alternative other than to follow him, and once she had he floored her completely by striding over to her sink and filling her kettle, telling her firmly, 'Sit down. I'll make us both a hot drink.'

Sit down. In her own home! How dared he boss her around like this? How dared he assume that she would *want* to be in the same room with him, never mind calmly sit down and drink tea with him? And yet his actions were so reminiscent of the easy relationship they had once shared . . . which she had *thought* they had once shared, she reminded herself grimly.

He was, she realised, removing two mugs from the open shelf above his head, and while she had fumed in silence at his high-handedness the kettle had started to boil. Unless she wanted to find herself drinking his damned tea she was going to have to find a way of making him leave.

'Tea-bags,' she heard him murmuring under his breath, and then, like someone watching disaster approach them in slow motion, she tensed as she saw him reach unerringly for the ugly pot pig sitting on its haunches on the shelf.

'You've still got this!'

Was that amusement she could hear in his voice or contempt?

'I intended to give it to one of the vicar's jumble sales when I moved in here, but somehow I felt he'd have been less than thrilled with it,' she told him with as much casual wryness as she could manage, while inwardly she was cursing herself for her idiotic sentimentality, not just in keeping the damn thing but also for having it on open display where he could so easily see it.

In her own defence, she could hardly have expected him to walk uninvited into her home, her kitchen, and coolly start making her tea.

'I remember the day I won it for you,' Gareth was saying softly. 'It was either this or a goldfish. I thought you'd opt for the fish. After all, that's what you'd said you wanted.'

'I know, but there was only one left, and that little boy wanted it so desperately. I could see it in his eyes.'

'Yes,' he agreed soberly. 'You always were a softie ... sensitive to the feelings and needs of others ... putting them first.'

For some reason his quietly spoken words made her feel uncomfortably vulnerable.

'I was a child,' she told him quickly. 'People change.'

'Some do,' he agreed, still with that same sober note in his voice, his eyes intent as he studied her. Looking for changes in her. She tilted her head proudly. Well, if he thought she was still that same sentimental child he had taken to the town fair ...

'They have to if they want to survive,' she added, and then flushed wildly, praying that he wouldn't sense the self-betrayal hidden within her words.

To her relief he didn't, instead saying curtly, 'Do you still take your tea without sugar?'

She nodded and watched as he poured the tea into two mugs, bringing one over to her.

'I meant what I said about owing you an apology, you know,' he told her sombrely. 'I was standing outside your partner's office this morning and I overheard what you were saying to her about Lewis. I should have known really... should have realised that you simply aren't the type to——'

'To what?' she challenged him. 'To arouse the desires of a man——?'

She stopped, biting her lip in vexation. What inner treachery had pushed her into making such a revealing comment? She paused, waiting for Gareth to pounce on it, to hold up to her her own admitted vulnerability, but to her confusion instead he said grittily, 'All right, I suppose I deserved that comment.' He gave a small shrug, the gesture so heart-stoppingly familiar that her reaction to it raced through her own flesh like an overdose of alcohol carried in the bloodstream. He was and always had been such a very male man, tall, powerfully built, with muscles honed from his love of being outside rather than developed in some arid expensive gym. She remembered once...she must have been about fourteen, or maybe even fifteen. She had gone round to the house and had found him bare-chested and knee-deep in the circular stone fishpond in the formal part of the Cedars' garden, cleaning out the weed that had been threatening to choke the lilies.

She could recall today, as intensely and as vividly as though it had happened only hours ago and not years, the sensations of raw aching love and longing which had engulfed her as she'd watched him, his torso brown and hard with muscle, his jeans slipping low on his hips so that her shocked and fascinated gaze had been able to trace the dark line of hair disappearing beneath his belt.

A peculiar sensation of weakness had filled her then, a burning heat combined with suffocating breathlessness...faintness almost, and then Gareth had come wading towards her, chafing her teasingly, threatening to lift her into the water to join him if she had nothing better to do than to stand and watch him work.

His teasing had broken the spell engulfing her, and the moment had been forgotten, pushed to the back of her mind until the next time she had become aware of him in the same way.

And now he was a man, and without knowing how she knew she did know that, beneath the expensive casualness of his clothes, his body would be now as it had been then: hard with muscle, satin-fleshed, with that same arrowing of fine dark hair which her fingers had ached to reach out and touch.

She shuddered inwardly. His very presence here in the same room as her was a reminder of so many things she would rather forget, resurrecting so many emotions she had thought safely destroyed.

Where another woman might have rejoiced in this confirmation of her sexuality, she wanted to reject it; to deny not only that she had ever felt that way, but also that she was still capable of doing so.

'Come back.'

The soft words startled Sybilla into focusing on his face. He was watching her with an oddly sombre expression in his eyes, his weight resting easily against the unit behind him as he leaned against it.

'You always were a dreamer... idealistic.' His mouth twisted suddenly. 'Perhaps I should have remembered that instead of allowing myself——' He stopped again and then said curtly, 'I still haven't apologised properly for the other night. You and I go back a long way, Sybilla. There was no reason why we shouldn't...'

'Be friends' was what he'd been about to say. Pain pierced her with all the sharp agony of a knife-point. The very last thing she wanted was

Gareth's friendship. It would destroy her to be forced to accept that kind of role in his life when she wanted . . .

When she wanted what? His love? No, of course she didn't. She didn't want anything from him . . . anything at all, and as for his claim that he wanted to apologise, that he wanted them to be friends, well, no doubt now that he was moving back here he wanted his life to run on smooth, even lines.

Once she accepted his apology, once she allowed him back into her life . . . She gave a fine shudder. No, she could not do that . . . could not allow herself, betray herself into that sort of emotional danger. It would be far safer to keep up her barriers, to hold him at a distance.

Much as she hated to admit it, she was still far too vulnerable where he was concerned.

'I don't want your apology, Gareth,' she told him stiffly. 'In fact, I don't want anything from you at all, other than that you stay out of my life.'

She couldn't look at him, but she heard the savagery of his indrawn breath and trembled inwardly. This was so unlike her, so diametrically opposed to her real nature, her real desires. Inside she felt as though she was tearing herself apart, but what alternative did she have?

Once before she had suffered the pain and anguish of hearing him deride her for her love for him, of hearing him reject that love as unwanted

and embarrassing. She was never going to allow
him to humiliate her like that again.

Terrified that her resolution might desert her,
that she might weaken and give in to the temptation to grasp the olive branch he was holding out
to her, she repeated quickly, 'I don't want your
apology, Gareth. I don't want it and I don't need
it. You see . . .' she took a deep breath and turned
to face him, praying that her courage wouldn't
desert her ' . . . you see, your opinion of me . . . of
my . . . my morals and the way I live my life means
nothing to me at all.' *You* mean nothing to me at
all, she wanted to add, but she simply could not
get her lips to form the words, and, dismayingly,
for some obscure reason she could actually feel
the small scar on her bottom lip starting to throb,
even though the pain of it had gone.

She held her breath, her body gripped by tension and pain, and then she heard Gareth saying
coolly, 'I see.'

She prayed that he did not; that he did not see
through the barriers she was trying to put up to
the real vulnerability she was trying to shield.

'I think perhaps, then, that I'd better leave.'

'Yes,' Sybilla agreed tonelessly, not daring to
look at him in case she gave in and begged him to
stay.

Good manners forced her to accompany him
to the door, but as he drew level with her she
flinched back from him, freezing when, instead

of politely responding to her desire to put more
space between them, he came closer to her, his
expression shadowed and unreadable.

'I've made my fair share of mistakes in my
time, but none that I regret more than...'

She couldn't bear it... couldn't endure him so
close to her. She felt both unbearably nervous
and sickly excited all at the same time, her stomach churning, her senses overwhelmed by the
sight and scent of him. Giddily she closed her
eyes, touching her tongue to her over-dry lips.

'Sybilla.'

The rawness in his voice sent her pulse accel-
erating wildly out of control. She opened her eyes
and discovered that he was staring at her mouth.

'Does it still hurt?'

For a moment, for one wild anguished moment she thought he was referring to the past;
that he had broken all the rules and was actually
bringing out into the open his awareness of how
she had felt about him; but then, as he reached
out and touched her bottom lip with his thumb,
she realised that he meant her mouth; that he was
asking her if her mouth still hurt.

'I never meant...'

His voice was rough and uneven, setting off a
chain of reactions inside her body. Helplessly her
lips started to part, her eyes huge and dark as
they reflected the shock of what he was doing to
her. His thumb brushed gently against the small

scar, his throat suddenly ridged with tension as he swallowed.

'Ten years ago you'd have wanted me to kiss it better for you.'

She stared at him in disbelief, unable to comprehend that he had actually spoken such words.

The huge aching ball of pain inside her splintered into a million diamond-sharp shards which tore into her nervous system, destroying her self-control, her defences, leaving her so emotionally vulnerable, so close to betraying tears that she could actually feel the hot sting of them in her throat and eyes.

His thumb was still resting against her mouth. Desperately she took a step back from him, bumping into the wall behind her, her face white with shock and distress, her voice croaky and unfamiliar as she told him huskily, 'Ten years ago I was a child... a fool, but I'm neither of those things now, Gareth.' And I don't know why you're trying to torment me like this, an inner voice cried out in anguish, but she refused to voice such words—to allow him to guess at the hurt she was trying to conceal.

Was this his way of punishing her for her refusal to accept his apology, by reminding her of how stupid she had once been?

'Please leave,' she demanded unevenly. 'I'm sure your...girlfriend must be wondering what's taking you so long.'

'My girlfriend?' Her heart sank as he picked up her words. Why on earth had she given in to that childish impulse to throw that at him? His private life . . . his personal relationships—these were nothing to do with her. Better by far for her to have preserved a dignified silence on the subject than to have descended to the level of throwing such a childish comment at him.

'Oh, you mean Lois. Lois isn't my girlfriend. She's my American attorney,' he told her crisply.

She could feel her skin burning with embarrassment and anger.

'I don't care what role she has in your life, Gareth,' she told him untruthfully. 'I merely assumed——'

'That she and I were lovers. Just as I assumed that you and Lewis . . . Dangerous things, aren't they, assumptions? Especially when they're fuelled by . . .' He paused and gave her a thoughtful look. 'What exactly were yours fuelled by, Sybilla?'

'Nothing,' she lied, aware of how dangerously unstable her position was becoming. 'As I've already told you, your private life is of no interest to me.'

'Oh, yes, you've certainly made that fact clear enough,' he muttered under his breath, much to her relief, as he turned towards the door.

He started to open it and then paused, turning back to her saying, 'You'll have heard, of course, that I've decided to move back here to take over the running of the business.'

Inwardly trembling, she still managed to give a very dismissive, casual shrug as she agreed as carelessly as she could, 'Belinda did say something of the sort.'

'But you weren't in the least bit interested,' Gareth broke in, his voice sharp with a bitterness she found impossible to understand. 'Yes, I think I've got the message now, Sybilla. Don't bother to walk me to my car. I'm sure you've a dozen or more far more important things to do,' he told her sarcastically. 'By the way, one final thing: the shaving-foam; since it obviously wasn't, as I'd supposed, for your lover, then . . .?'

She was too astonished to lie.

'It . . . it was for my neighbour's husband. I was doing some shopping for them. They're elderly and——'

She stopped. Why on earth was she explaining herself to him like this? And why on earth had he assumed the shaving-foam must mean that she had a lover, a relationship intimate enough to necessitate her purchase of such an item? But before she could ask him he was walking away from her. She told herself that she wasn't interested in his reply anyway. He obviously liked jumping to the wrong conclusions about her. Because he wanted to believe that she had a lover and that he was safe from her unwanted love for him? Well, he need have no fears on that score. None at all.

An hour after he had gone Sybilla was still trembling in the after-shock of his visit. It was no use now telling herself that the sane and mature thing to do would have been to accept his apology, to be calm and businesslike with him, cool and distant, instead of allowing her emotions to run riot and cause her to behave so self-betrayingly and foolishly.

Fortunately he hadn't seemed to realise that her rejection of his apology sprang more from fear, for a need to protect herself than from any desire to snub or reject him. But once he had calmed down... once he had had time to think over their interview, might he not realise the truth?

What made her think he would bother to spend time going over their conversation? she derided herself scornfully. Did she honestly believe that he was like her, that he would waste hours and hours obsessively examining every word she had spoken, every nuance of expression and emotion? No, of course he wouldn't. He would simply shrug off her refusal to accept his apology, tell himself that he had done the right thing in tendering it and put her right out of his mind.

He didn't really care whether they got on cordially together or not, and she certainly wasn't

going to allow him or anyone else to start remembering the past, to start remembering how
she had once hung on his every word, gazed at
him with adoration and love, and to start watching her reaction to him with amusement and
contempt, looking for all those small signs of
self-betrayal made by those who had the misfor-
tune to fall desperately in love with someone who
could not love them equally intensely in return.

No, better by far to hold him at a distance, to
be cold and remote towards him, than to risk the
kind of danger she knew instinctively would
come from accepting his apology...his offer of
'friendship'.

It was very much later that she realised that as
a businesswoman her first thought ought not to
have been for her own emotions but for the possible harm she might have done to the business by
rejecting his apology, but it was too late now for
second thoughts. He wouldn't be coming back to
apologise again. Not after the reception she had
just given him.

She knew that knowledge ought to be reassur-
ing and satisfying, but instead it made her feel
unbearably unhappy and alone. She sneezed and
then cursed under her breath. If only she felt
better physically she was sure she would be in a
much stronger position to deal with this unwanted emotional vulnerability which had sur-
faced to frighten and confuse her.

Was it really only a week or so ago that, if asked, she would have immediately and confidently stated that Gareth meant nothing whatsoever to her now?

Had it really only taken one meeting and one angry, intense kiss to show her just how she had been deceiving herself? Was she really such a fool?

It seemed that she must be, she admitted later, curled up in bed, acknowledging what she had been trying to deny to herself ever since she had looked up in the car park and seen him there. She still loved him.

She twisted restlessly in her bed, telling herself that it couldn't be possible; that at fifteen, going on sixteen, she had been a child, capable not of love but only of adoration; of hero-worship; that she had seen Gareth as a god whom she had elevated to a pedestal far, far beyond her own reach.

Now she was an adult, and adult love involved emotions that meant meeting as two equals, emotions which allowed the other person to be human, to have faults; love meant accepting a person as he or she really was, not transforming them into someone superhuman, super-perfect, which was surely what she had done with Gareth. She had fallen in love, as teenagers did, with an ideal, an ideal created by her own mind, her own imagination, her own needs and longings. She had not known the real Gareth at all.

But no, that wasn't true. She *had* known the real Gareth, and she had known him for far longer than she had been infatuated with him. She had known his kindness to her as a child, his compassion... his concern... his consideration. She had known the innate gentleness of his nature, the true kindness that extended to include everyone around him. He had teased her at times, it was true, but it had been a gentle, warm teasing, without malice or cruelty, and until she had overheard that betraying conversation and shut herself off from him, denying herself any kind of access to him, he had given her a great deal of his time... his attention.

All through her childhood she had treated the Cedars as a second home and Gareth himself as a cross between an older brother and a favourite cousin. No, she could hardly claim that she did not know him.

And yet he had changed, must have changed to have misjudged her so quickly and so angrily. The Gareth she had known would never have done that.

And these feelings she still had for him, feelings which, for lack of any other fitting description, she was forced to call love... How could she say with one breath that she loved him, and yet feel with another such a fierce anger and resent-

ment towards him for all the havoc he was causing in her life?

So what was she saying? That, because she was
angry, hurt, even bitter towards him, she could
not love him? So what were her feelings, then...?

Were they merely physical...lustful...left-over
embers of a teenage sexual curiosity which should
have died out years ago, but which for some unfathomable reason his reappearance had fanned
into white-hot life.

Because she *did* desire him; she couldn't deny
that. This evening, standing in her kitchen,
watching him, she had been overwhelmed by
feelings of such a physical intensity that the
memory of them even now, when she was alone,
made her tremble with a mixture of guilt and anger.

So was it just an inconvenient physical desire
she felt for him, and, if her sexual feelings were
so easily aroused, why was it that no other man
had aroused them?

It was true that she had deliberately shielded
her emotions, deliberately guarded her heart,
afraid of allowing any man to get too close to her
in case he, like Gareth, rejected her; and, because she was the person she was, she had always
assumed that for her physical desire must go
hand in hand with emotional desire, that she was
not a woman who could ever separate the two.

And if that was true then this unwanted, aching desire she felt right now must mean . . .

She rolled over, pulling her pillow over her head and groaning out load. Why was she tormenting herself like this, like a masochist, hooked on self-inflicted pain? Why didn't she just admit the truth instead of torturing herself? She loved Gareth. She *must* do . . . otherwise why was she so desperately afraid . . . why was she so determined to remain cold and distant with him? He had wanted to apologise for misjudging her, but she had refused to let him. She had almost actively encouraged and fed his hostility towards her.

Why? Surely not merely out of stubborn pride, because she was determined that never again would he have a reason to deride her feelings for him.

If only he had stayed safely out of the way in America. If only he had not decided to return home.

She pushed away her pillow. She was aching all over with tension and fear. If only she could close her eyes, go to sleep and then wake up to find that the whole thing had been only a nightmare.

Her throat was sore with unshed tears, and she smiled grimly to herself, remembering a much younger self who had cried herself to sleep night after night for weeks on end after overhearing Gareth's conversation with his grandfather.

Well, she wasn't going to fall into that trap this time. This time. This time she was a woman, not a child. This time no one would be allowed to guess what she was feeling, least of all the man responsible for those feelings.

What she needed, she decided fretfully, thumping her pillow and trying to get comfortable, was something to take her mind well and truly off Gareth Seymour.

CHAPTER SIX

IN THE morning Sybilla was forced to admit the veracity of the old saying about being careful about what you wished for in case you got it.

Her throat felt as though it had been scraped raw and was now on fire. Her head ached so badly that the pain made her want to scream— only that would have made her throat worse— and her body felt as though every muscle and piece of bone had turned to sponge overnight, and a sponge, moreover, filled with a hundred and one niggling aches and pains.

She would feel better once she was in the office and concentrating on her work, she assured herself grimly as she dosed herself with a couple of aspirin and a mug of coffee.

When she got to the office, Belinda took one look at her and told her forthrightly that by rights she ought to be at home and in bed.

'But, knowing how stubborn you are, I suppose it's no use my telling you that.'

'None at all,' Sybilla agreed. 'I'm far too busy to be ill,' she added jokingly, but in truth the last thing she wanted was to be at home on her own with time on her hands to think about Gareth.

For a while the aspirin she had taken first thing helped to alleviate her symptoms a little, and later, while they were quiet, she nipped out of the office and headed for a nearby chemist.

'Got the bug, have you?' the chemist asked her gloomily as she explained what she wanted. 'None of this stuff can cure it, you know,' he added, indicating the rows of preparations on the shelves behind him. 'Flu is flu, and——'

'I just want something to alleviate the symptoms,' Sybilla interrupted him quickly.

Ten minutes later she emerged from the shop, carrying a bag containing something to ease her sore throat, something to relieve her aches and pains, and something for the congestion in her chest, but she knew, as the chemist had already pointed out to her, that none of them could offer her a cure and would only provide temporary relief from her symptoms.

If she could just keep going until after the silver wedding party. She had to go to that.

She had almost reached the office when she saw Gareth coming down the road towards her. He saw her almost at the same time as she saw him.

Both of them paused and exchanged brief, grim glances. Without waiting to see if he intended to acknowledge her, Sybilla turned on her heel and walked into an adjacent newsagents, where she bought a magazine she didn't really want before emerging and finding to her shock that Gareth was standing on the pavement outside, almost as though he had been waiting for her.

'Is this going to be a regular occurrence?' he demanded angrily, putting out a hand to detain her when she would have walked past him. 'Because if so——'

'I don't know what you mean,' Sybilla told him untruthfully, and then sneezed so violently that she had to stop speaking.

Immediately Gareth's frown deepened. 'Are you completely crazy?' he demanded bitingly. 'You're obviously not well. You——'

'I've got a cold, that's all,' Sybilla snapped at him, 'and if you're worried about catching it then I suggest you let go of me.'

They were, she realised, attracting a good deal of attention from passers-by. It was only a small town, where virtually everyone knew everyone else, and she was uncomfortably aware that Gareth's eyes hadn't been the only ones to notice all those years ago how much she had idolised him. She had no wish to fuel fresh gossip and speculation. She had the business now to consider, after all, and its standing in the local community. It wouldn't do her credibility as a businesswoman any good at all if people started believing she was still mooning around after Gareth.

Still holding on to her arm, Gareth told her, 'I bumped into the Gittingses the other day. I hadn't realised that they were celebrating their silver wedding this year. They were telling me that your parents will be at the party. It will be good to see them again.'

Sybilla's heart sank. That meant that Gareth would be attending the silver wedding party. If only she could find an excuse not to go, but that was not only impossible, it was also something she simply could not do. Paul Gittings was her godfather. She had to be there.

She moved back automatically as a woman pushing a pram came towards them, and Gareth moved with her, somehow or other coming to stand much closer to Sybilla than he had been doing before.

'Will you be going to the party on your own...or...?' He paused and looked at her.

'No, I won't be going alone,' she told him acidly.

It was, after all, quite true. She would be going with the rest of the family, but she knew quite well that that wasn't what Gareth had meant. Would she be going with a man—that was what he had been asking her—a lover? Grimly she wondered how he would like it were she to pry into his private life in the same way, and then de-

GET A FREE TEDDY BEAR...

You'll love this plush, cuddly Teddy Bear, an adorable accessory for your dressing table, bookcase or desk. Measuring 5½" tall, he's soft and brown and has a bright red ribbon around his neck—he's completely captivating! And he's yours *absolutely free,* when you accept this no-risk offer!

AND FOUR FREE BOOKS!

Here's a chance to get **four free Harlequin Presents® novels** from the Harlequin Reader Service®—so you can see for yourself that we're like **no ordinary book club!**

We'll send you four free books...but you never have to buy anything or remain a member any longer than you choose. You could even accept the free books and cancel immediately. In that case, you'll owe nothing and be under **no obligation!**

Find out for yourself why thousands of readers enjoy receiving books by mail from the Harlequin Reader Service. They like the **convenience of home delivery**...they like getting the best new novels months before they're available in bookstores...and they love our **discount prices!**

Try us and see! Return this card promptly. We'll send your free books and a free Teddy Bear, under the terms explained on the back. We hope you'll want to remain with the reader service—but the choice is always yours!   106 CIH AK9E (U-H-P-11/93)

NAME

ADDRESS   APT.

CITY   STATE   ZIP

Offer not valid to current Harlequin Presents® subscribers. All orders subject to approval.
© 1993 HARLEQUIN ENTERPRISES LIMITED   **Printed in U.S.A.**

▼ CLAIM YOUR FREE BOOKS AND FREE GIFT! RETURN THIS CARD TODAY! ▼

NO OBLIGATION TO BUY!

cided to risk his anger and give him a taste of his own medicine.

'And you?' she asked with a false smile. 'I expect you'll be taking your... attorney?'

'Lois? Hardly. She flew back to Boston this morning. Once she realised that I intended to stay on here there was no point in her remaining. In reality she's the company attorney. They sent her with me in the hope that she'd persuade me to stay on with them, but my contract was up for renewal anyway, and once I realised the state the company was in...' He paused, and when she looked questioningly at him he explained tersely, 'Gramps was an astute businessman in his time, but recently... well, let's just say that the business couldn't have been sold as a going concern, and to close it down would have meant putting too many people out of work. I'm still not sure I'm doing the right thing, at least not from a purely businesslike point of view, but emotionally...' He gave a brief shrug, while Sybilla stared at him in astonishment that he should be so open and frank with her.

This was the old Gareth. The Gareth she remembered with such aching nostalgia and pain. The Gareth who could never bear to inflict pain on others.

'Sentiment is never a good basis on which to found a successful business,' she told him, more crisply than she had intended because that was the only way she could hold at bay the emotion she was feeling inside.

Instantly he released her arm, so quickly that the loss of the warmth of the contact with his body actually made her give a small forlorn shiver, her body missing the bulk and comfort of his as he stepped away from her.

'There speaks the successful businesswoman,' he derided sardonically. 'Funny how things change . . . how people change.'

'Yes, isn't it?' she agreed equally acidly, and then started to walk away from him without formally saying goodbye.

It was only when she reached her own office that she allowed herself to stop and turn round, to watch as he walked down the street away from her, her vision blurred by the tears she was fighting hard not to let fall.

Why couldn't he leave her alone? Ignore her . . . pretend she just did not exist as he had done in those agonising months when she had first realised that he didn't want her, when she had first decided to cut him out of her heart and her life?

Later that day, as she gave in to her aching body's need for an early night, Sybilla reflected that the only good thing to come out of the day had been her interview with their prospective new temp. His skills and qualifications were excellent, and their only problem was going to be keeping him on their books as a temp. All too soon one of their clients would be bound to offer him a permanent position.

'So you're meeting your family there at the club?'

'Well, it seemed the sensible thing to do,' Sybilla informed Belinda. 'They won't be able to stay very long. Anthony will need to leave fairly early and, since Mum and Dad are travelling with them, it seemed silly for them to waste time by driving to my place first.'

'What are you going to wear?' Belinda asked her. 'Something new?'

Sybilla shook her head. 'No, I haven't had time to buy anything. You know how busy we've been lately. I thought I'd wear the black dress I bought just before Christmas.'

The dress in question had been expensive; far more expensive than Sybilla had intended. She had bought it for the local Chamber of Commerce dinner-dance, having seen it in a small boutique on a visit to the city.

It was a designer model, the salesgirl had told her, and had been reduced because of its small size, but, even reduced, the price-ticket had made Sybilla gasp a little. However, once she had tried the dress on, she had been forced to admit that the luxurious matt-black jersey, the cut and style of the dress, the way it fitted and enhanced her slender frame, did put it in a class of its own. The only trouble was that she hadn't been sure if she could actually afford that particular class. In the end she had closed her eyes and told herself that if she starved for the rest of the month and made do with last year's black velvet pumps she could probably just about afford it.

'Mm. You'll look stunning. There's something about the combination of a little black dress and a diminutive blonde...'

'I am not diminutive and neither am I blonde,' Sybilla retorted acerbically.

'No,' Belinda teased her with a grin. 'Tell that to that husband of mine! A week after the Chamber of Commerce do he was still drooling.'

To her own embarrassment, Sybilla knew that she was blushing, which made Belinda's grin widen even further.

'Mind you, if you are planning to wear that dress, what you really need is a good accessory,' Belinda mused.

'Thanks, but furs and diamonds aren't my style,' Sybilla told her.

'I wasn't actually thinking of furs or diamonds, more along the lines of a tall, dark and handsome male escort,' Belinda corrected her.

Her description came so close to fitting Gareth that immediately Sybilla over-reacted, almost snapping at her friend, 'Thanks, but no thanks. I might be well into my mid-twenties, and I might not have a man in my life...a husband or lover... but that doesn't mean that I'm not perfectly happy and contented with my life just the way it is. In fact——'

'Hey, hang on! You've got the wrong end of the stick,' Belinda interrupted her easily. 'I wasn't suggesting you needed a man in that sense. I was thinking more in the way of a bodyguard.' She gave a rich laugh. 'To judge from my normally very restrained husband's reaction to that black dress, without one you're going to spend most of your evening fending off the majority of the male guests.' She paused and added more soberly, 'Look, I'm sorry if I offended you. I never meant to suggest...'

Sybilla bit her lip. What on earth had possessed her to over-react in that silly way? Of course Belinda hadn't meant anything by her comment and she ought to have known it. It was true that Belinda had a good sense of humour and liked to tease her occasionally, but her teasing was always kind and gentle and she never objected to being teased back in return.

'No, *I'm* the one who's sorry,' Sybilla told her apologetically. 'I don't know what's got into me today... it must be this cold. But I hope you're wrong about the dress.' She paused, and added uncertainly, 'Perhaps I ought to wear something else.'

'Don't you dare. Think of how much it cost,' Belinda added wickedly. 'You can't afford not to wear it really, can you?'

'No, I suppose I can't,' Sybilla agreed drily, but a couple of hours later, standing in front of her bedroom mirror, surveying her appearance, she frowned as she wondered what on earth it was about the dress that was likely to provoke the male reaction threatened by her friend.

It was long-sleeved, with an admittedly slightly *décolletée* neckline but only slightly. True, the matt-black jersey did mould her body as though it had been made to do so, but since it was also ruched and draped it could hardly be described as skin-tight or even mildly provocative. Could it?

Blind to her own feminine appeal, she couldn't see the allure of the paleness of her skin highlighted by the density of the black jersey... just as she couldn't see that the soft ruching with its delicate hinting of the curves it concealed was far, far more provocative and enticing than a more raunchily styled dress could ever have been. Nor did she realise that the way the neckline was styled so that it revealed virtually all of the soft sweep of her shoulders might incline a man to wonder just how much gentle pressure it would take to cause the soft fabric to slide free of her shoulder altogether—perhaps no more than the simple physical movement of taking her in his arms, thus leaving her silky skin open to the exploration of his hands . . . his mouth.

A man might see all these possibilities at a glance, but Sybilla was oblivious to them. Belinda must have been exaggerating, she decided frowningly as she studied herself from every angle, assuring herself that there was nothing remotely provocative in her appearance and that she needed not fear being castigated by the other guests for turning up dressed in something vulgar and unsuitable.

Perhaps it was because she wasn't really used to wearing dresses that she felt so vulnerable in this one. Suits and separates were more her style, plain, unfussy businesslike clothes of a type that impressed their clients and reflected an aura of efficiency and practicality.

Certainly no one could ever describe her dress as practical, nor the sheer black silk tights she was wearing with it. Even her shoes had higher heels than she normally favoured.

She picked up her evening-bag and headed for the stairs. She was, as she had already told Belinda, meeting her family at the country club where the party was being held. They had all contributed to a joint present and so she had nothing to take with her. Giving her appearance one last fleeting look, she walked towards the door, hoping grimly that the medication she had just taken would see her through the evening.

She wasn't really sure she was wise to be driving, but she promised herself that she would be very sparing in her alcoholic consumption in view of the drugs she was using, even while her conscience pricked her guiltily that she ought perhaps to leave her car and instead ring for a taxi.

Unfortunately it was too late for that now. The town's single taxi firm would be fully booked for the evening, and if she was late her parents would start worrying.

She shivered a little as she stepped outside. It wasn't particularly cold, but the evening air felt raw and damp, and a sudden fit of shivering struck her as she got into her car.

Tomorrow was Saturday, she reminded herself unsympathetically, and she would have the whole weekend ahead of her during which to indulge in the misery of her cold; for tonight she would just have to continue to fight it off.

Determined to maintain this uncompromising attitude, she started the car engine and reversed into the road.

The Gittingses had hired one of the private function-rooms at the club in which to celebrate their silver wedding, and as Sybilla walked across the car park towards it she could tell from the level of noise inside the room that she would be far from the first to arrive.

Her host and hostess welcomed her fondly as she walked in through the door, complimenting her appearance, her godfather remarking in an avuncular way that it didn't seem five minutes since he was holding her over the font.

'Your parents are over there with Anthony and Claire,' he told her.

Thanking him, Sybilla made her way across the dimly lit room to the table in question.

'Darling, how nice you look,' her mother enthused as she kissed both her parents.

'Yes, very sexy,' her brother teased her, grinning at her.

Even though she knew that Tony was only teasing her, a small *frisson* of doubt still quivered down her spine. *Was* there something about the dress which she just could not see, something that made it give onlookers a totally erroneous impression of her?

Reading the doubt in her eyes, her sister-in-law quickly reassured her.

'Take no notice of him, Syb. You look terrific. You always look elegant and well-groomed, but this dress makes you look softer...more approachable——'

'As I said, it's sexy,' Tony interrupted his wife irrepressibly. He added, 'What would you like to drink, Syb? It's my round, so...'

'Just mineral water,' she told him, quickly explaining, when he frowned, about her cold and the medication she had taken.

'Darling, I'd no idea you weren't feeling well,' her mother told her. 'I hope it is just a cold and not this dreadful flu that seems to be going around. It's practically decimated the village, hasn't it, Claire? Luckily, as yet we've all managed to keep clear of it.'

'This isn't flu, Mother,' Sybilla told her firmly. 'It's just a boring dull old cold.'

'Well, if you're sure——'

'Stop fussing, Ma. She's all grown-up now,' Tony interrupted, coming to her rescue as he got up to attract the attention of one of the circulating waiters.

'Looks as if Rita and Paul have invited practically the whole town,' he commented once he had ordered Sybilla's mineral water, making Sybilla's heart sink as he added, almost accusingly, 'You never said anything about Gareth Seymour deciding to move back and take over the family business. I was speaking with him earlier. From the sound of it, he's going to have quite a challenge ahead of him. He's going to have to totally re-equip, and he wants to modernise—install the latest computer technology. Nice chap. I've always liked him,' Tony added musingly. 'Although you were always closer to him than I was.'

Sybilla felt her stomach muscles tightening with tension, but her brother had been away at university the summer she had made such a nuisance of herself, had humiliated herself so dreadfully, and so had never actually realised what had happened.

'See much of him, do you?'

'Not really.' Her abrupt answer caused him to pause and look at her, a tiny frown appearing between his eyebrows as they darkened with brotherly concern.

'Syb,' he began, but Claire leaned forward, touching his arm, asking him if the couple standing several feet away were, as she suspected, old friends of his parents who had been guests at their wedding.

Had Claire intervened deliberately tactfully, deflecting his attention, or had her timely intervention simply been a fortunate accident?

Telling herself that she was being too sensitive, that it was hardly likely that Claire knew how much of a fool she had once made of herself over Gareth, she turned to her parents, explaining to them that she was hoping to be able to make definite arrangements to take some time off and spend a week with them very soon.

'Well, I think you should have some kind of break, darling,' her mother told her worriedly. 'You've lost weight, and you're looking rather peaky.'

'Thanks!' Sybilla laughed.

'You mustn't overdo things. You work so hard.' Her mother paused and gave a faint sigh, and Sybilla knew what she was thinking. Proud though she was of her business success, she would have liked her to settle down...to marry and have children.

Well, she wasn't against the state of marriage, and as for children...she was very fond of her brother's two and enjoyed the time she spent with them. However, when it came to taking a more personal view of marriage...

She doubted that she would ever want to let any man close enough to her emotionally to allow their relationship to develop to the point where marriage became a viable proposition.

Lost in her own thoughts, she didn't see Gareth approaching their table until he stopped beside it and exclaimed, 'Mr and Mrs Gardner! How nice to see you both.'

'Gareth! Tony said he'd been talking to you. I believe you've decided to move back here permanently. We were so sorry about your grandfather. Are you here on your own? Why don't you join us?'

Sybilla froze, wishing herself a thousand miles away. Why on earth hadn't she thought of this possibility? Her mother was so open and friendly with everyone; she had known Gareth all the time he was growing up; Sybilla should have guessed that once she saw him she would want to catch up on all his news.

Gareth, though, was bound to refuse her invitation.

But, to her horror, instead she heard him saying easily, 'Well, if you're sure I shan't be intruding...'

'Of course not.' As he sat down, her mother went on, 'I don't know if you've met Claire, Tony's wife?'

'No, I haven't.'

A small sharp pain speared Sybilla's heart as she watched the way that Gareth smiled at her sister-in-law and saw her immediate feminine response to it. No woman could fail to respond to Gareth when he smiled in that fashion. His smile was so warm, so genuine, making it easy to respond to him, and yet there was nothing practised or deliberate about it.

'I was just telling Sybilla that it's time she had a break. She's lost weight and now this cold...'

Sybilla knew that her mother wasn't deliberately drawing Gareth's attention to her, but nevertheless she shrank back into her chair and avoided looking at him, willing him to realise that this enforced intimacy between them was none of her doing...that it was not at her instigation that he had joined her family.

'She does look a little fine-boned,' she heard Gareth agreeing equably, tactfully responding to the maternal concern without falling into the trap of implying that she looked either haggard or unwell, Sybilla noticed cynically.

'But then, she's always had that very feminine air of fragility about her, hasn't she? I wasn't surprised when Gramps left her the Dresden. He once told me in a moment of weakness that whenever he looked at the more delicate of the shepherdesses they made him think of Sybilla, and I know what he meant.'

Everyone had gone silent; her mother, Sybilla noticed, was looking faintly pink and bright-eyed, while Tony's jaw had dropped.

'Steady on, Gareth,' he expostulated. 'Are we talking about the same Syb that I remem-ber...the one who broke both her arms climb-ing trees or, rather, falling out of them...the one who fell into the fish pond at the Cedars so often that Dad swore she was going to grow fins?'

Tony's indignant comments had broken the silence that had followed Gareth's extraordinary remark; everyone was laughing...everyone apart from Gareth and herself, Sybilla noticed. He was looking at her in a way that was making her heart beat double its usual rate and her breath lock tightly in her throat. Was that really how he saw her: as fragile and delicate as a piece of Dresden china? But no...it couldn't be. If he had, he would never——

'How come you're here on your own?' Tony was asking Gareth curiously. 'I heard that you arrived in town accompanied by a stunning female.'

'Lois Friedman, an attorney who works for my American employers. My contract with them was up for renewal and she came over with me to try to give me a helping hand in sorting out any complications that might have arisen from Gramps's will from the American legal side of things. The transfer of any assets over there, that sort of thing.

'Once I'd made the decision not to return but to stay on here there was nothing to keep her here. She flew back to Boston the other day.'

Nothing to keep her here. That was the understatement of the year, Sybilla reflected acidly. From the way she had seen Lois clinging possessively and determinedly to Gareth's arm that morning in the car park, the woman had thought she had a *very* good reason for being with him.

Had she been sitting with anyone other than her own family, Sybilla would have found some excuse to get up and leave, but how could she?

If only Gareth would make some excuse and leave, but he seemed perfectly content to stay where he was, exchanging reminiscences with her parents, telling them about his plans for the future of the business, turning to her far too frequently to draw her into the conversation . . . but she stubbornly stayed aloof, answering his questions monosyllabically, even though she knew her behaviour was drawing surprised and concerned glances from the rest of the family.

It was only when it was announced that the buffet meal was now ready that she felt able to give a small sigh of relief, but this relief quickly turned to anxiety when Gareth turned to her mother and asked, 'Would you mind if I ate with you? I seem to have lost touch with so many people while I've been away.'

'Of course you must stay with us, Gareth.' Her mother beamed. 'I expect you and Sybilla must have a lot to catch up on. Such a shame that, whenever you came home, Sybilla was away,' she continued innocently.

'Yes, a very great shame,' Gareth agreed.

Sybilla couldn't look at him. He must have realised long ago that she, armed with advance information of his visits from his grandfather, had deliberately made arrangements to be out of town herself when he came home. Not out of pique, but out of a desire to reinforce to him that he need have no fears that she would ever, ever again embarrass him and humiliate herself in the way she had done the summer she was fifteen.

'Never mind,' her mother was saying cosily. 'Now that you're home for good there'll be plenty of time for you to catch up on each other's news.'

'Plenty,' Gareth agreed urbanely, and Sybilla wondered if she was the only one to notice the sardonic look he gave her as he turned his head and murmured quietly to her, 'plenty of *time*, but, it seems, very little opportunity.'

Sybilla assumed that the buffet meal was up to the club's usual high standard, but what little she could manage to eat tasted of absolutely nothing at all. Her lack of appetite must be due to the medication she had taken and her still very sore throat, she consoled herself as she pushed her food round her plate. It couldn't possibly have anything to do with Gareth's presence at their table, and, contrary to what he had said to her mother, it seemed to her that people remembered him very well indeed, to judge from the number who came up to their table to talk with him.

She was glad that her family had decided to leave early because, she acknowledged, medication or not, she was beginning to feel distinctly unwell.

The toasts were drunk, the speeches given, the cake cut, all through which she had to endure Gareth's presence at her side, his suit-covered arm constantly rubbing against her body as he raised his glass or clapped the speech-makers.

When the men had gone up to the buffet to fill everyone's plates, on their return Gareth had

taken Tony's seat next to her, although she felt
confusingly sure that somehow or other the chair
was now far closer to her own than it had been
when her brother had been occupying it.

After supper the band started to play dance
music. Ignoring the increasing soreness of her
throat and the aching in her joints, Sybilla
danced with her godfather, her father and her
brother, and then inevitably came the moment
she had been dreading when, out of good manners, Gareth had no option other than to ask her
to dance.

And she, of course, had no option other than
to accept, with her family looking on.

Shakily she made her way on to the now
crowded and dimly lit dance-floor and then
turned to face Gareth, her eyes bright with defi-
ance, a hectic flush burning her face.

So far she had managed to avoid coming into
any kind of physical contact with him, with-
drawing from him the moment his arm brushed
hers at the table, making sure she took the drink
he was handing her from him without having to
touch his fingers, but now, as he took her in his
arms, her physical reaction to him was so strong
that her whole body actually shook with the force
of it.

'You're trembling,' he told her, frowning down
at her.

'I'm shivering, actually,' she fibbed.

'In here?'

The derision in his voice increased her defensiveness.

'I do happen to have a cold—remember?'

Instantly his attitude changed. He stood still on the dance-floor and to her shock reached out and placed his cool fingers against her hot forehead, exclaiming frowningly, 'You're running a temperature. By rights you shouldn't be here.'

'I've got a cold, not bubonic plague,' she taunted acidly, 'but if you're afraid of catching it from me then I suggest——'

'So that's what this is all about. Tell me something, Sybilla: why is it that you're so afraid? Every time I come anywhere near you, you back off from me.'

'And you find that surprising? What am I supposed to do? Throw myself into your arms and ?' She stopped abruptly, her face hot, chewing miserably on her bottom lip.

'Hardly.'

Sybilla told herself that it was only her own fault if the harsh, clipped denial held an obvious distaste for her suggestion. After all, what had she expected? She knew already what he felt about her.

Tears burned her throat and the backs of her eyes. It must be her cold that was making her feel so emotionally vulnerable, she told herself desperately.

The band was playing a slow romantic number; couples were drifting round the floor held close in one another's arms. Once, the thought of dancing with Gareth in such circumstances would have dazzled her with the promise of the unimaginable delight of being held in his arms, close to his body, and yet, now that the fantasy was a reality, she was doing all she could to hold herself as far away from him as possible without letting either Gareth himself or anyone else become aware of her rigid tension.

And yet what, after all, was there to fear—that if she relaxed her guard and allowed him to hold her closer he would somehow be able to divine her real feelings, that he would register the furious beat of her heart, know her body's aroused aching for him, feel as she did herself the fluid softness threatening to invade her muscles?

But how could he really know any of these things? Her body's secrets were her own and could not possibly be guessed at by anyone else, at least not with the double protection of their clothes to come between them.

Her face started to burn with anger and guilt as she recognised the wanton direction of her own thoughts, the images with which they were subtly trying to undermine her determination to refuse to allow her love for Gareth any kind of expression.

Bitterly she closed her eyes, wanting to blot out his face, but, behind the darkness of her shuttered lids, her imagination tormented her with the very thoughts she had been trying to deny, with images of the two of them together, his body sleek and powerfully male, his skin smooth and warm, his hands caressing her, tenderly at first, gently almost, and then with increasing passion, until——

'Sybilla, are you all right?'

The sharp question broke into her fantasy, shattering it. She opened her eyes and focused on Gareth's face.

'You aren't going to faint are you...? For a moment——'

'I'm fine,' she lied shakily. 'I just don't——'

'Want to dance with me. Yes, I do realise that,' he interrupted her bitingly. 'You have already made that more than clear. What the hell is it with you, Sybilla?'

His anger broke through her protective defences, making her give him a bitter, scornful look.

'Do you really need to ask?' she challenged him. 'How do you expect me to behave towards you, Gareth?'

She realised suddenly that the band had stopped playing and that people were starting to leave the floor. Abruptly she pulled away from him, heading back to her parents.

'Darling, are you sure you're all right?' her mother asked anxiously as she sat down. 'You look so flushed. Are you sure it isn't the flu?'

'Stop fussing, Mum,' Sybilla begged tiredly. 'It's a cold, that's all.'

'Well, if you're sure,' her mother said doubtfully. 'Tony was just saying that it's about time for us to leave.'

'I think I'll join you——' Sybilla started to say, but her mother protested immediately.

'Oh, no, darling, please don't. I feel bad enough that we're all having to leave so early, and Paul is your godfather. If you're worried about being on your own I'm sure Gareth...'

Sybilla felt her face burn with vexation and embarrassment. 'No, I'm not worried about that. I'm sure Gareth has other people he wants to spend some time with.'

She knew that Gareth was standing behind her and that he must have heard her mother's comment, and the last thing she wanted was for him to feel that good manners dictated that he stay with her after the rest of her family had gone. If only she could leave with them. Her whole body felt as though it was on fire, every muscle, every joint aching feverishly. Her throat was so sore that she could barely swallow, and as for the pain in her head ...

'We'd better go and say our goodbyes. Now, you will ring us soon, won't you, darling, to let us know just when you're able to come over?'

As she kissed her family goodbye Sybilla was acutely conscious of Gareth's presence immediately behind her. She was as sensitive to it as though his body gave off an extra-special heat to which hers was acutely responsive. If only he would go away. But she was being too impatient; once her family had gone ...

'Would you like another drink?'

His quiet mundane question caught her off guard. She turned round to look at him and then said acidly, 'There's no need to continue the pretence any longer, Gareth.'

'And what pretence is that?' he demanded as she started to turn away from him, taking hold of her wrist, forcing her to remain where she was.

'The pretence that you actually want to spend time in my company,' Sybilla threw at him, suddenly too weak and too miserable to control her feelings any longer.

There was a pause during which Gareth searched her face, his glance penetrating and thorough.

'And what makes you think it's a pretence?' he asked quietly, still watching her.

Sybilla could feel the colour come and go under her skin. Angrily she wrenched herself out of his grasp.

'*You* might enjoy playing these kind of games, Gareth,' she told him wearily, 'but I'm afraid I don't. And now, if you'll excuse me, I think it's time I had a word with my godfather.'

As she walked quickly away from him she prayed that he wouldn't come after her. She had had just about as much as she could stand. She had no idea what was prompting his behaviour, whether it was some machiavellian desire to hurt and taunt her, or whether he was genuinely oblivious to her desire to keep as much distance between them as possible, but what she did know was that her self-control was wearing perilously thin.

She spent fifteen minutes or so chatting with her godfather and his wife and then excused herself, explaining that she wasn't feeling very well and apologising for leaving so early.

'That's all right, Sybilla. You mother said it looked as though you were about to go down with this wretched flu,' Rita said sympathetically.

So much for her belief that she had convinced her mother that it was only a cold, Sybilla reflected ruefully.

She hadn't brought a coat with her, so there was nothing left for her to do other than head for the exit and slip quietly away.

She was very proud of the way she managed to stop herself from pausing by the door and turning round to allow herself one last masochistic look at Gareth.

All she had to do now was to get herself into her car, drive herself home and then thankfully get herself into bed. Wryly she admitted that in her present state she perhaps ought not to be driving, but it was too late to worry about that now. She had no alternative, had she?

Five yards or so away from her parked car, she froze, instantly recognising the man leaning against the driver's door, arms folded across his chest as he watched her approach.

Gareth! What on earth was he doing by her car? How had he known she had left? *Why?*

'Gareth,' she protested weakly, putting a hand to her head, trying to clear her muzzy, confused thoughts.

CHAPTER SEVEN

'THAT'S right, Gareth,' he mimicked savagely, unfolding his frame from the side of Sybilla's car and coming towards her, saying dangerously, 'I do hope you weren't thinking of driving yourself home, Sybilla.'

Immediately she flared back angrily, 'And if I was what business is it of yours?'

'I do happen to be a fellow road-user,' he told her drily, 'and as such I resent my life being imperilled by the potentially dangerous driving of someone who is not only under the influence of drugs, but who is also too stubbornly stupid to see that in her present physical state she has no right to be behind the wheel of a car at all.'

For a moment she was too surprised to speak.

'Joined the police force now, have you?' she taunted him angrily. 'Well, for your information——' The deep wrenching shudder that tore through her prevented her from continuing with what she had been about to say.

She tried to evade him as he came towards her, but couldn't summon the energy to move so she was grasped firmly by the upper arms and dragged within inches of his body as he demanded brusquely, 'Don't be a fool. You're shivering so much you can hardly move, never mind drive. Do you honestly think I'd let you drive yourself home in this state? Do you think anyone responsible would? I'll take you home.'

'But my car——' she started to protest weakly.

'To hell with your car. Look, I'll arrange to have it picked up and brought back to you in the morning,' he told her, refusing to let go of her as she struggled to push him away.

'I can't let you do this,' she told him almost fretfully, tears not very far away. It seemed so unfair that, after all she had done...after all she had put herself through, fate was forcing her to endure his company like this... forcing her into a situation which it must know she simply did not have the self-control to cope with.

'*Letting* me doesn't come into it,' Gareth told her derisively. 'Now, are you going to walk across to my car or do I have to carry you?'

Before she could say a word he muttered something under his breath that she couldn't quite catch and then told her brusquely, 'On second thoughts, carrying you will probably be quicker and simpler,' and then before she could stop him he was swinging her up into his arms, causing her to cling wildly to his dinner-suit jacket as a wave of dizziness attacked her.

She tried to tell him to put her down, but somehow the words became lost, confused by the opposing commands given out by her brain and her heart.

Make him stop...make him put you down, her brain ordered, but her heart, her body, her senses...traitorously they whispered to her that wasn't this, after all, what she wanted, what she had yearned for?

Treacherously they urged her to give in to the temptation to relax in his hold, to curl her body into the protective warmth of his, to close her eyes and absorb the long-familiar and long-ached-for scent of him, to place her free hand against his heart. It was beating faster than it should, she recognised, and then acknowledged that even her small frame was still quite a weight for a man to carry and was doubtless responsible for the increased tempo.

When they reached his car he put her down beside the passenger-door, easing her slowly and carefully to the ground and holding her, sup-ported—or imprisoned, perhaps—within the curve of his left arm while he used his right hand to unlock the door.

The seats in his car were far more comfortable than those in hers, she acknowledged tiredly as she closed her eyes and leaned back against the head-rest.

Beside her, Gareth put the car in motion, its engine smooth, almost soundless.

He was a good driver, but that was something she had already known.

She remembered his first car. His grandfather had paid half the cost of it and Gareth had saved the other half from a summer job between leaving school and going on to university. A bright yellow Mini, she had affectionately been named 'Pudding', partly because of her shape, he had explained to an admiring Sybilla, and partly because she was custard-yellow.

She remembered the first time he had taken her out for a drive, how proud and excited she had felt. How grown-up, despite the fact that her hair had been in plaits and she'd been wearing white socks and Clarks school sandals.

Unknowingly her mouth had curved into a soft reminiscent smile. Seeing it, Gareth demanded harshly, 'Whoever you're thinking about obviously appeals to you far more than I do.'

His comment caused Sybilla to open her eyes and turn her head to stare at him in surprise.

For a moment he had almost sounded . . . resentful. . . bitter. . . jealous. . . but that, of course, was impossible.

'As a matter of fact I was thinking about Pudding,' she told him, honestly too surprised to contemplate evasion. 'Remembering how thrilled I was the first time you took me out in her.'

'Pudding.' Gareth's mouth curled into a smile. 'Mm. Those were happy times. A pity that——'

'That they had to end. That I had to go and spoil everything,' she challenged bitingly. 'What did you expect, Gareth—that I would stay a child forever?'

She closed her eyes again, turning her face away from him, not really surprised that he didn't make any response to her angry accusation. After all, what response could he make? They both knew the truth.

With her eyes half open, the engine humming almost silently, the darkness of the night all around them, the confines of the car forced an intimacy she would have preferred not to experience. Although she tried not to give in to the temptation to do so, her body was already moving restlessly, forcing her to turn in Gareth's direction so that she could see the way his hands rested on the steering-wheel, the way the fabric of his trousers pulled against the muscles in his thighs when he changed gear.

Humiliation scalded her that she should be so physically aware of him, so filled by the aching need to reach out and touch him, to smooth her hand along his thigh, to experience for herself the taut strength of his body, to feel the warmth of his skin beneath her fingertips, the softness of his body-hair, to...

She swallowed the whimper of anguish burning in her throat as her body responded to the provocation of her own thoughts, the ache low down inside her gathering and intensifying, the tightness of her nipples causing them to swell and harden, to push against the soft fabric of her dress, so that when she moved protestingly in her seat, restlessly trying to blot out what she was feeling, she inadvertently dragged the silky-textured fabric against her own body, the friction causing the ache in her breasts to intensify.

Out of the corner of her eye she saw that Gareth was looking at her, and colour bloomed on her skin as she suppressed the urge to take a hasty downward look at her own body just to reassure herself that he could not possibly have seen the hard thrust of her nipples, concealed as it was by the soft ruching of her dress.

Was there some male instinct, some male sixth sense that alerted a man to the fact that a woman found him physically desirable even when there was no outward evidence to prove that fact?

She was surely letting her imagination, her dread of his discovering how she felt, what she was enduring, frighten her with danger that could not possibly exist.

Even so... She moved uncomfortably in her seat, turning away from him, acknowledging that, for some rebellious reason, this action seemed to intensify all her aches and pains, so that it seemed her very joints were linked in some conspiracy to undermine her. Even her throat seemed to ache more when she turned this way. But what was an aching throat when compared with the humiliation of Gareth's recognising her physical arousal and knowing that he was the cause of it?

'Are you all right?' His quiet question broke the silence between them.

'No, I'm not,' she told him almost crossly. 'My throat's sore, I ache all over, and——'

'And you say you've only got a cold,' he derided her, interrupting her. 'What on earth possessed you to come out tonight anyway? By rights you should have stayed at home in bed.'

'And spared you the necessity of having to endure my company. I only wish I had.'

She gasped as the car came to an abrupt halt and Gareth turned to her, reaching out and taking her arm, holding her imprisoned as he said savagely, 'Right, that's it. I've had just about as much of this as I can stand. Why the hell do you keep accusing me of not wanting your company? *You're* the one who's spent the last ten years avoiding mine. *You're* the one who's made a point of being out of town whenever I was likely to come home. *You're* the one who's literally crossed the road to walk on the other side rather than speak to me. And why, for God's sake? Why?'

Sybilla stared at him. She was trembling, she discovered absently, whether from shock because he was still touching her or from the force of the anger building up inside her, she had no idea.

'You can ask me that? You *know* why, Gareth. You *know* quite well why I've spent the last ten years avoiding you. All right, so at fifteen I thought you were a god among men. I worshipped the ground you trod... I even fancied myself in love with you, but that was a child's fantasy. It's over now,' she lied, unable to look at him. 'I do realise how... how you felt...' She stopped, her voice suspended, unable to go on, unable to reveal to him her knowledge of how irritating and unwelcome he had found her adoration and love.

He was silent for so long that she risked a look at him. He had released her arm and was sitting rigidly in his seat, staring out of the window into the darkness.

'You *knew*. I never... Yes, now I do understand,' he told her, and oddly his voice was very bleak. 'I suppose that should have occurred to me, for I thought foolishly that I'd kept my feelings to myself, that you didn't——'

'Please, I don't want to talk about it,' Sybilla interrupted him huskily.

'And I take it that we can't be... friends.'

His question stunned her, making her throat ache not with pain, but with suppressed tears. For a moment he had sounded almost humble...almost pleading...but that surely must be her imagination working overtime again.

She couldn't summon the words to respond and could only shake her head, eventually saying thickly, 'No, I don't think I could...'

She couldn't go on...couldn't tell him that she just did not believe she had the will-power to endure his friendship where she wanted his love...that sooner or later she was bound to betray to him what she felt, and that once she had done... Well, the situation was embarrassing enough as it was.

Some sensation, some awareness of him making a move towards her made her flinch back from him, dreading his contempt, his pity, and she froze when she heard him curse under his breath.

'For God's sake, Sybilla, don't make it worse for me than it already is.' And then unbelievably he was reaching for her, taking her in his arms, ignoring her gasped protest, her shaky whispering of his name as he closed the gap between them and told her broodingly, 'You aren't fifteen any more, Sybilla, and this isn't forbidden between us now.'

His words were whispered against her lips. She knew he was going to kiss her, but what she did

not know was why. Out of pity... out of anger... out of some emotion she could only try to
guess at as she fought to stifle the pain burgeon-
ing inside her, the need to turn her face and plead
with him not to torment her like this... not to
hurt her by giving her something which could
never be anything more than a pale shadow of the
intimacy she really wanted.

She tried to say his name and discovered that
she couldn't because his lips were already caressing hers, exploring their shape slowly, lingering,
while his hands slid into her hair, gently support-
ing her head.

This was a dream. It had to be. This couldn't
possibly really be happening, and yet it was.
There was no way she could have imagined the
sensation that shot through her as his tongue-tip
found the small wound on her bottom lip that he
himself had inflicted.

'Sybilla.' He said her name slowly, achingly, as
though he was savouring it, his tongue-tip exploring the shape of her mouth, causing her flesh
to burn and her bones to melt.

Somehow, and she didn't know how or when
it had happened, her hands had slid beneath his
jacket and were pressed flat against his chest. He
moved one with his free hand, urging her to slide
it around him and then, as its twin followed suit,
he closed the gap between their bodies.

She shuddered as the need inside her bolted out of control, closing her eyes, curling her fingers into his back, stifling a small sob at the back of her throat as he moved and the friction of his movement caused her swollen nipples to throb unbearably.

'Gareth, please,' she begged him.

'One goodbye kiss, a formal ending to our old relationship. It's something we both need,' he told her harshly, and she knew she couldn't deny it, couldn't deny him, even though her heart ached over that word 'goodbye'.

His hand touched her face, cupping her jaw, his thumb stroking the corner of her mouth and then her bottom lip. She could hardly breathe, her body ached so much, but not now with the kind of pain that came from her cold.

This ache was caused by the overwhelming need she felt for him ... the almost uncontrollable desire to take hold of his hands and place them on her body, to show him ... beg him ...

She made a small inarticulate sound of distress, flinching as his gaze focused on her, his eyes brilliant and dark.

She tried to pull away from him but her sleeve caught against one of the buttons of his jacket as she tried to withdraw her arms from his body, pulling the neckline of her dress so that it slid completely free of her shoulder.

She wasn't wearing a bra underneath it—the dress's boning made it unnecessary—but now, as she saw how much of her body was revealed, she wished that she were. Now having slid free of her shoulder, the neckline of her dress was gaping to show not only the soft swell of her breast, but also the taut and swollen nipple that crowned it.

She took a deep shuddering breath, her body tight with anguish and shame, trying desperately to pull away, to turn her head, but Gareth's hand against her jaw held her captive, her eyes huge and dazed with the conflicting confusion of her emotions as she realised that he still intended to kiss her . . . that . . .

'Gareth . . .'

Her intended denial became a soft whimper of mind-destroying pleasure as his mouth touched hers, not, as it had done before, in anger . . . but with warmth and gentleness, his kiss explorative, delicate, slow, as though he wanted to take the time to absorb every minute sensation from the tremulous satin-softness of her outer lips to the betraying moistness of her mouth itself.

And all she could do was to cling helplessly to him, drowning in the rip-tide of passion that was storming through her.

When his tongue parted her lips and the gentleness of his kiss turned to passion she stopped trying to tell herself that she ought to resist, and instead gave way to the anguished need tormenting her body, clinging to him, responding to him, answering the passion he was giving her.

When his hand touched her breast it wasn't alarm bells that rang inside her, but a fierce, wild clarion peal of delight. Her body was no longer prepared to listen to the urgings of her mind, to its plea for caution, for care. It felt no shame, no danger in allowing Gareth to know how much his touch pleasured it.

She heard him groan, felt the shift in weight of his body and then its aroused hardness as he pushed down the top of her dress and cupped her naked breasts with his hands, stroking her erect nipples while he continued to kiss her with an intimacy she had never imagined experiencing.

This was not Gareth the god whom she had put on a pedestal. Neither was it Gareth the distant cold stranger, nor even Gareth the angry contemptuous enemy. This was another Gareth . . . a Gareth her senses had always told her must exist, but a Gareth who until now had been a stranger to her.

When his mouth left hers and started to explore the soft slope of her shoulder her response was immediate, her nails digging into the hard muscles of his back, her breasts swelling, her body trembling with eager anticipation.

Gareth was trembling too, or was that merely her imagination?

A low moan of pleasure was dragged from her throat, her whole body convulsed by a shudder of delight as his tongue stroked her nipple, circling it, bathing it in a moist heat.

'Gar...eth...' She couldn't help herself. She moaned his name in a helpless plea for the pleasure he was withholding from her, a soft whimper of anguished delight emerging from her throat when he started suckling on her breast, gently at first, slowly and tenderly, and then, as though he realised the intensity of her need, far less gently so that the pleasure he gave her made her whole body shudder over and over again.

When he released her breast and gathered her closely against him, kissing her mouth with the kind of passion she had never remotely imagined experiencing, she stopped trying to analyse what was happening and why and simply gave herself up to the delirium of it.

It was the bright lights of an oncoming car that finally brought them both to their senses, causing them to break apart, Sybilla's face flushed and strained with tension, Gareth's dark and set as he apologised tersely, 'I'm sorry. That should never have happened. I never intended——'

'Look, please just take me home,' Sybilla begged him, tugging her dress back into place, unable to bring herself to look at him as she turned towards the darkness outside the passenger window.

'Sybilla——'

'Please. I don't want to discuss it, Gareth. As you just said, it should never have happened. Now will you please take me home?'

She was so close to breaking-point. She felt as though her very bones would break under the strain of it. Dear God, what on earth had she *done*? He must know now how she felt about him. How she still felt about him after all these years. It was different for a man. He could experience passion, desire... physical arousal with a woman for whom emotionally he felt nothing at all. He was not a fool, she knew that.

She could only pray that he would be as anxious as she was herself to put what had just happened between them right out of his mind.

After this she didn't know how on earth she was ever going to be able to face him again. How she was ever...

She tensed as the car stopped, flashing him a quick anxious look. He wasn't looking at her, she realised, and no wonder.

It was only when he offered curtly, 'If you'd like me to come inside with you and check...' that she realised they were parked outside her house.

Quickly she assured him, 'No. I'll be fine.' She was already struggling with the door-handle, desperately anxious to get away from him before he started thinking that she was deliberately delaying in the hope that... That what? she asked herself self-castigatingly. That he might kiss her again...touch her again...caress her again. She took a deep breath, and half fell out of the car as the door finally opened.

Gareth had, she noticed, switched off the engine, and as he too made to get out of the car she protested quickly, 'No, please stay where you are, Gareth. There really is no need.'

'If that's what you prefer.'

His voice was terse; clipped. He wasn't looking at her, she recognised without surprise. He must be nearly as embarrassed as she was herself, although for very different reasons. He must be cursing ever having offered a lift. What on earth was wrong with her, letting a simple kiss between two friends get out of hand like that . . . practically inviting him . . . begging him almost? She shuddered hotly, conscious of a wave of humiliation burning her inwardly and out.

All she wanted to do was to escape from him, to be on her own, to come to terms with the folly of her behaviour.

'Sybilla——'

'No, Gareth, please just leave me alone.'

She almost ran up the path to her front door, her fingers trembling as she inserted the key into the lock. Once inside, she closed the door and then locked it, leaning heavily on it as she waited for the sound of Gareth's car driving away. Only once she had heard it did she make her way slowly and painfully upstairs.

CHAPTER EIGHT

IT WAS the racking sound of her own coughing that woke Sybilla up; her throat was so sore that she could barely swallow, her eyes felt gritty and hot and her body ached all over. She shivered under the bedclothes, muzzily torn between going downstairs to make herself the soothing drink her throat cried out for and staying right where she was, closing her eyes as tightly as she could while she curled up under the duvet into a tight defensive ball, retaining what body-heat she could.

In the end the pain in her throat won out. Shivering, she crawled out from under the bedclothes, dismayed to discover how weak she felt, how unsteady her balance was as she walked towards the bedroom door.

Halfway down the stairs she was seized by such an intense bout of shivering that she had to cling on to the banister rail to prevent herself from falling.

In the kitchen she opened the fridge and suddenly realised that her fresh milk must still be outside. She unlocked the door and retrieved the two pints from the doorstep. The night held that quality of dense silence that always seemed to occur in the hour or so just before dawn. Less than a mile away, Gareth would be lying in his bed at the Cedars. Would *he* be thinking of *her* ... remembering how ... ?

This time when she shivered it wasn't with cold but with self-revulsion.

How could she have allowed her guard to slip so devastatingly? How could she have been foolish enough to actually ... ?

She tried to swallow but her throat was too swollen and sore. She felt too ill to dwell on her disastrous behaviour with Gareth, and as she ransacked her fridge, finding the three lemons she had vaguely remembered seeing there the last time she'd opened the salad box, she tried not to admit the uncomfortable suspicion that the dramatic acceleration in her illness from a heavy cold to full-blown flu might be a bit of determined coat-trailing on the part of her body in its attempt to escape from the third-degree inquisition it might otherwise have been subjected to by her brain.

Her brain! And what exactly had that been doing while she had been flinging herself headlong into danger ... headlong into Gareth's arms? Sleeping? Turning a blind eye? Why hadn't *it* reminded her, protected her? Why had *it* allowed her to behave so foolishly...so...?

She winced as the lemon she was squeezing dripped some juice into a tiny cut on her finger, licking it off and instantly grimacing at its bitterness.

Was she crazy, she asked herself despairingly, wandering around her kitchen at three o'clock in the morning, making herself a hot lemon drink to ease a sore throat which common sense had already told her could only properly be treated by either time or a course of antibiotics?

If she had any sense at all she would take a couple of aspirin and go back to bed, and pray that when she woke up the events of the evening would have been wiped from her mind completely. And from Gareth's.

Sighing, she was forced to acknowledge that this was unlikely to happen. The best she could hope for was that Gareth, who would surely have as little desire to dwell on which had occurred as she had herself, would follow her example and ensure that in future they met as infrequently as possible.

What hurt her the most, she acknowledged as she stirred her drink and then sat down on a chair, sipping the hot liquid, was that she had been so confident, so sure that she was safe...that the past and her adolescent love for Gareth were no longer of any importance...that, no matter how much pain they had caused her, she was past that pain now and that there was no way she could be hurt by Gareth again.

It had taken her less than ten seconds in his arms tonight to realise how wrong she had been. Ten seconds...the time it had taken for his mouth to brush hers, for the heat of his body...for the touch of his hand——

She gave a sharp exclamation of pain as the hot liquid slopped out of the mug and scalded her skin. As she put the mug down she realised she had been trembling so much that she had caused the lemon drink to spill.

The best and safest place for her was in bed, she told herself firmly, holding on to the mug with both hands while she drank the contents, and then going back upstairs.

Once she was back in bed, though, she found it was impossible to sleep. Every time she closed her eyes she was immediately tormented by mental images of Gareth. Not the familiar Gareth of her adolescent daydreams, but a new, older, more mature and infinitely more disturbing Gareth...a Gareth whose kiss, whose touch wasn't merely the emotional fantasy of her teenage yearnings...but instead had a reality, a substance that no amount of imagining on her part could ever have conjured up.

*   *   *

She couldn't remember a Saturday that had ever made her feel more alone, more of an alien in a world of couples and happy families, Sybilla reflected miserably as she unpacked her shopping.

She wasn't sure if it was the virus that was making her feel as though even her bones were cold and aching or if the wind had been as raw and demoralising as she had thought.

She didn't even want to think about how much of her intense inner sense of coldness could be attributed to the realisation that she was still as much in danger from her emotional vulnerability to Gareth as she had ever been, perhaps even more so.

Her hands shook a little as she unpacked the fresh bread she had collected from their local bakery.

There had been a man standing in the queue in front of her, two small children, obviously his, clinging to his side.

He had been about Gareth's age, although nothing like as physically compelling as Gareth... even so, to see the way his two small daughters clung so adoringly to his side had brought a lump to her throat and had made her body ache in a way which was totally unfamiliar to her.

She had looked round the bakery then, and it had seemed to her that everyone else was in pairs, in family groups, that she was the only person there on her own; and she had suffered such an acute and overwhelming surge of loneliness that she had had to grit her teeth and will herself not to give way to the tears of self-pity she had felt threatening to flood her eyes.

What on earth was wrong with her? She had never minded being alone before, never even given it a passing thought. After all, over the years there had been more than enough men who would have gladly changed her single state had that been what she'd wished.

But she had not done so... had not wanted a partner... a lover... commitment... home... children. Until...

Until Gareth had taken her in his arms, had kissed her and touched her, and even though their lovemaking had stopped short of complete intimacy it had still left her with an unfamiliar ache within her body, an ache not just for him as a man—as her lover—but an ache for all that loving him meant she could never have.

Standing there in the bakery, watching that unknown man with his daughters, she had suffered such an overwhelming sense of loss, of emptiness, that its echoes still tormented her now.

She moved restlessly around her kitchen. Outside, the sun was shining even if the wind was cold. If she had any sense she would put on her outdoor clothes and go outside and do some much needed digging. The physical exercise would soon help to banish her unhappy mood, and the fresh air would probably do her good.

Could fresh air cure her malady? She doubted it!

Gareth had been as good as his word, and when she'd woken up and gone downstairs she had discovered that her car was parked neatly outside its garage.

She wondered what time he had driven it back; she had certainly heard nothing. She tried to tell herself that she was glad that she hadn't had to endure the humiliation and embarrassment of seeing him, but inside she still ached... still yearned... still *loved*, she admitted tiredly.

She looked through the window and out into the garden. The sun was gone now, the blue sky turning grey as the sharp spring wind whipped up the rain clouds.

Her phone rang and she went to answer it, her heart beating rapidly and shallowly, but when she picked up the receiver it was her mother's voice she heard—enquiring anxiously if she was feeling any better—and not Gareth's.

Gareth. Why on earth had she thought it might be Gareth? She had already told herself that the last thing she wanted was any kind of contact with him. It was too potentially humiliating... too potentially dangerous.

She didn't have the emotional resources to cope with the physical reality of him, not after having so newly discovered that she loved him.

She loved him. Her mouth twisted bitterly. What a cruel, unfair stroke of fate had brought her full circle like this to find herself face to face with exactly the same heartache she had suffered at fifteen.

No, not exactly the same; then pride, youth and resilience had been on her side. Now...

Now she knew with heartaching certainty that, unlike her physical illness, her love for Gareth was a malady from which there was no hope of recovery.

Having put away her shopping, she admitted that, sensible though it might be for her to go outside and do some work in the garden, what she really felt like doing was curling up in a chair in front of the fire with a cup of tea and one of her ancient and very well-read Georgette Heyers to make her both laugh and cry and to give her an escape route for a short space of time.

She unearthed one of the books from the back of a cupboard, lit the sitting-room fire and filled the kettle.

Later she decided that the reason she didn't hear Gareth's car was because she was wallowing so deeply in self-pity, but by then it was too late to look for excuses: the damage was done.

It happened just as she was reaching for her tea-caddy, or rather for the china pig Gareth had won for her all those years ago, and which she had cherished ever since, preferring—for a reason which was unhappily no longer obscure to her—to have an excuse to touch the object every day than to store it away somewhere where she might have to give herself an excuse to do so.

Perhaps her hands were still too cold, or perhaps they were slightly damp, she didn't know; all she did know was that the shock of seeing Gareth walk past her kitchen window just as she was reaching for the pig was enough to cause her to let the heavy china slip from her fingers and crash down on to the terracotta floor-tiles.

Of course, she knew that it would break, but that didn't stop her diving to catch it and then staring in distress at the broken shards of china when she'd missed.

'Sybilla . . . what happened? I heard a crash.'

She must have left the door unlocked, she acknowledged numbly, refusing to turn round, unable to turn round as she continued to survey the mess on the floor. China mingled with split tea-bags, and, even though common sense told her that the jar was far too badly smashed to ever be repaired, she discovered that she was down on her hands and knees, frantically trying to extract the pieces from the rest of the disorder.

It took Gareth's sharp, 'Don't touch it, you could cut yourself. Where do you keep your brush?' to make her realise what she might be betraying to him, causing her to kneel back on her heels, keeping her back towards him, as she responded as evenly as she could.

'It's all right, Gareth. I'll deal with it.'

She could hear the tension in her voice, feel the sharpness edging up under it, a sharpness she was using to mask the despair and distress she was suffering.

That pig had been something she had cherished ... a gift from Gareth to a much younger Sybilla, but a gift given with affection ... with even, perhaps, love, although admittedly not the love of a man for a woman. She had cherished that pig ... had loved it ... and now it was gone. Broken ... destroyed by her own clumsy carelessness, and in part by Gareth himself.

She could feel the hot tears of pain burning behind her eyes. There was nothing she wanted to do more than to stay where she was on the floor and give way to her grief, howling like a small child with a bloody knee, to cry the tears now she had never allowed herself to cry before ... but Gareth was here ... standing behind her ... watching her ... and suddenly, briefly, she hated him almost as much as she loved him, getting up and turning on him to demand angrily, 'What is it you want, Gareth?'

He literally stepped back from her as he registered her anger... her rejection, a subtle tightening of the bones in his face sending warning signals to her own brain, reminding her that there were more ways than the obvious of betraying one's true feelings.

'I just came round to check if you were OK. After last night.'

The blood literally seemed to freeze in her veins. How could he do this to her? If she had expected nothing else from him she had hoped that he would at least have the courtesy, the compassion never to mention what had happened between them last night, either to her or to anyone else, but to tactfully blank it off, to pretend that last night... that her responsiveness to him... her desire for him... her love for him had never existed; and yet here he was, walking into her kitchen, carelessly asking her if she was 'OK'.

A sick feeling of light-headedness swept over her, a mingling of anger and pain, and as she turned away from him she said as steadily as she could, 'Why on earth shouldn't I be? I *have* been kissed before, you know.'

The words had an acid ring to them, a bitterness that shocked her. A terrible silence followed them, an awareness burning through her that she had said totally the wrong thing.

'Yes, I should imagine you have,' Gareth agreed lightly. 'However, it wasn't that I was re-

ferring to. You weren't in evidence earlier on
when I returned your car. I had to pass here on
my way home, so I thought I'd call in and check
that you were all right.'

Each word was delivered lightly and without
emphasis, in complete contrast to her own
scornfully acid statement, and yet she knew...oh,
how she knew that, beneath his apparent outward calm, Gareth was furiously angry.

She was starting to feel sick again, but not this
time because of her virus. No, this time her nau-
sea was the result of pure gut-churning fear, she
acknowledged shakily. This time her sickness was
a direct result of her own idiocy.

What on earth had possessed her? Surely
common sense should have warned her that the
last thing Gareth would want to do was to refer
to what had happened between them last night,
that he would have as much desire to put the
whole incident behind him as she had herself?

He was still standing behind her, showing no
sign of leaving; there was only one thing to do.
Taking a deep gulp of air, she walked over to the
cupboard where she kept her sweeping brush,
opened it and removed the brush, and then,
keeping her head down as she swept up the mess
from the floor with fiercely short strokes, she
muttered huskily, 'I'm sorry. That was...that was
childish of me...but as you can see...' she paused
and looked briefly at him and then back down at

the floor before finishing '...I'm not in the most rational of moods this morning. In fact I was just about to make myself a cup of tea and go and curl up in front of the fire with an old Georgette Heyer.'

'A sovereign remedy for a fit of the sullens,' he commented, giving her the brief heart-catching smile she had once known so well. It made her heart shake and her throat ache as she fought the urge to drop the brush and run headlong into his arms and once there to give way to a good old-fashioned cry.

'Look, Syb, about last night; I did——'

She could feel her body tensing, rejecting what she knew was going to come. The typical embarrassed-male admission of having been carried away by sexual desire, of having made a mistake...of wanting to apologise for any misunderstanding.

'Please don't say anything,' she interrupted him. 'It was a mistake. We both know that. I don't want to talk about it, Gareth, and if you don't mind I'd like you to leave.'

The barrier between them, which had fallen so briefly when he'd teased her about her love for her Regency romances, was firmly back in place. She kept her back towards him, telling him with her body language that he wasn't welcome, no matter how much doing so might be tearing her apart inside.

She heard him open the door, and she held her breath.

'I'm sorry... about the pig.'

It was like a blow to her heart. Did he know how much that cheap piece of china meant to her? How often over the years she had looked at it and seen his face... heard his voice... felt the warmth of his hands... the sound of his laughter? And now it was gone.

Without stopping what she was doing, she told him curtly, 'It doesn't matter. I should have thrown it out years ago.'

She heard the door close but didn't turn her head to watch him walk away from her... perhaps for the last time... didn't stop her ritualistic, almost compulsive sweeping of the floor until she had heard his car start and was sure he had gone.

Then and only then did she drop the brush and get down on her hands and knees, slowly picking up every last piece of broken china, her tears mingling with the mess on the floor as she placed each piece on the table.

Hopeless to ever imagine it could be repaired. It couldn't. Just like her broken heart.

Stop being so melodramatic, she told herself fiercely, and for goodness' sake go upstairs and wash your face, you idiot.

Leaving the china, she did so, grimacing as she studied her tear-blotched reflection in her bathroom mirror.

Because the water was running and because the house was old, with sturdy stone-built walls, she didn't hear the kitchen door open as Gareth walked back in.

He stopped short, staring at the carefully placed pieces of china on the table, and then walked over to them, studying them, touching them.

A tender, rueful expression softened his face. He touched one shard thoughtfully, and then glanced towards the open inner door.

He had come back on impulse, driven by a need he didn't like to admit even now after all these years, an excuse for his return ready.

But now...

But now he needed time to think... to assess, to try perhaps to convince himself that it was foolish and extremely dangerous to allow himself to become so buoyed up by hope simply because of a few broken pieces of china.

All these years and nothing had changed. All these years of wanting... of hoping... of hearing from his grandfather only things he had not wanted to hear. And then to come back and find that there was no one in her life who... All right, so last night had been a mistake. He had let his heart rule his head, had given in to his own needs, his own yearnings... but perhaps after all the situation was not as irredeemable as he had feared...

A woman who would carefully sift through the mess presently adorning Sybilla's kitchen floor just to rescue the broken shards of a piece of china, that at best couldn't be worth more than a pound or so, couldn't be entirely indifferent to its giver... could she?

'Quit while you're ahead,' he urged himself as he heard a sound from upstairs, quietly reopening the door and letting himself out, but not before he had extracted one of the largest pieces of the broken jar and taken it with him.

When Sybilla came back downstairs she had the oddest feeling that someone had been in the house, and yet she couldn't understand why.

Shrugging, she finished cleaning up the mess on the floor, telling herself miserably that now not even the delights of Georgette Heyer would be sufficient to lighten her despair.

By Saturday teatime, sick of her own company and the unhappiness of her thoughts, which seemed to have created an atmosphere that hung over the house and her like a miasma of misery, she rang her mother and invited herself round to spend a few days with her parents.

Belinda, when she telephoned her later to warn her that she would not be in the office until the middle of the week, assured her that she could manage and told her that she was relieved that she was at last behaving sensibly and putting her health before the business.

An hour later, as she drove past the closed gates to the Cedars, she tried not to look in the direction of the house even though she knew from experience that it was impossible to tell whether or not a car was parked outside because of the banks of rhododendrons lining the drive.

Just the act of driving past the house was enough to increase her pulse-rate, to make her heart thud more heavily, and why? Just because Gareth was living there again—that was why.

One thing was becoming increasingly clear to her and that was that if Gareth did intend to take on the responsibility of the family business and stay in the area then she would have to move away—for the sake of her sanity if for nothing else.

What she hadn't decided was how on earth she was going to break this news to Belinda, what excuse she was going to use to explain why she was turning her back on all the years of hard work involved in setting up the business, and to do what?

Chewing on her bottom lip, she wondered if she had the acting ability, the sheer strength of will to convince her friends and her family that the time had come for a change... but a change to what? She could perhaps pretend that she wanted to be closer to her family, that she was thinking of establishing a new branch of the business close to them, but since they lived less than half a day's drive away that seemed hardly feasible. So what excuse could she give? Perhaps to Belinda she could bring herself to admit the truth and tell her the real reason she had to leave the area. Belinda would understand...would sympathise...but... She shook her head tiredly and scolded herself for not concentrating on her driving. Her reactions were far from being acute at the moment and this road, like all modern busy roads, would be extremely hazardous for the unwary driver.

She reached her parents' home just in time for supper, after which she was speedily dispatched to bed by her mother, who insisted on providing her with a soothing hot-water bottle and what looked suspiciously like her old teddy bear, plus a hot lemon drink which, Sybilla ruefully admitted, tasted far better than her own concoction.

'Try to get some sleep, darling,' her mother begged her. 'You look dreadfully worn down and far too thin. Something else isn't bothering you, is it? The business?'

'The business is doing fine, Mum,' Sybilla assured her, relieved to seize on this and so avoid the necessity of a direct lie. 'Mm. I do feel rather sleepy,' she added less truthfully.

Sighing faintly, her mother took the hint and stood up, pausing by the door before opening it and switching off the light. There was something, she knew it, as surely as she knew that

pressing Sybilla to confide in her would achieve
nothing. That was the trouble with grown-up
children: one still worried as much about them as
one had done when they were small, but once
they were adult their sorrows and pains could no
longer be soothed by a loving hug and a kiss.

No, whatever was bothering Sybilla was obviously something she preferred to deal with on her
own. But, whatever it was, it must be
serious . . . very serious for her to come home like
this. Normally she was so independent, stubbornly so at times. Even as a teenager, when she
had been going through that adolescent crush on
Gareth . . .

Sybilla's mother paused thoughtfully on the
stairs for a moment before going down them to
rejoin her husband in an extremely sober and
anxious frame of mind.

In the end, Sybilla spent three days with her
parents, giving in to her mother's cosseting and
to the boisterous visits of her brother's children,
letting herself sink down into the comforting
feather-softness of her family's love, deliberately blocking out each and every thought of
Gareth that tried to torment her.

Here at least there were no memories of
him . . . no fears that she would turn a corner and
come face to face with him. Here at least she was
safe from the past with all its tormenting memories and from the future, which had begun to

haunt her with its spectre of all the loneliness that lay ahead for her.

One day Gareth would marry, she was sure of that, and when he did ... She gave a tiny shudder, ignoring the imperious frown on her eldest nephew's face as she stopped reading from the book she was holding.

How was she going to live with that...with the reality of his marriage...his wife...his family...his happiness...while she...? She gave another tense shudder, causing Jack's frown to change to a sudden quick anxiety as he reached out to her and asked, 'Aunt Syb, are you all right?'

The anxiety in the small voice drew Sybilla's attention to his face. Conscience-stricken, she quickly assured him that she was fine. She had no right to inflict her heartache, her misery on the children, who were far too young to understand what was wrong with her. Sombrely she acknowledged that she couldn't hide herself away forever, burying her head in the sand like an ostrich, refusing to face facts. The best thing she could do, the only thing she could do was to go back, to tell Belinda honestly and openly why she felt she had to leave, and then to formulate some kind of positive plan for her future. What she needed was to give herself ... to find for herself something to cling on to...some kind of life-raft to support her through this time in her life when she felt she no longer had the strength to support herself.

If only Gareth hadn't returned none of this would have happened, she reflected bitterly, or even if he had come back, but she had known that his return was only temporary, that he would be going back to America . . . that, if she could only just manage to hold out for a short space of time, he would be gone and her life would return to normal; she could concentrate on forgetting him, on blotting out any mental image of him, of rejecting him from her life and her heart, but how could she do that now?

Part of her wanted to hate him for what he was doing to her, even if it was done in ignorance, even if he did not know. Did she want him to know . . . did she want him to realise . . . did she want his pity . . . his contempt?

She shuddered violently. No, of course not . . . her pride, her self-respect—they were all she had left, even if they were wearing dangerously thin, even if they were precious little protection against the agony of loving him.

No, she couldn't stay here with her parents forever. She must go home. She must see Belinda, and she must put her life in order, so to speak.

She left on Wednesday morning, despite her mother's plea to her to stay a little longer.

'The virus has almost cleared up now,' she responded truthfully. 'And it isn't fair to leave

Belinda on her own...not when we're so very busy.'

Reluctantly her mother let her go, standing anxiously by the garden gate until her car had disappeared before turning to her husband to remark worriedly, 'I hope she's going to be all right. Perhaps if I rang Gareth and——'

'You'll do no such thing,' Sybilla's father told her sternly, adding in a more gentle voice, 'You know that wouldn't be right...nor fair...to either of them.'

'No, I suppose you're right, Jeff. Oh, but I hate to see her like this. She looks so...so wretched.'

'I know, love. I know.' He patted her arm as they walked back to the house together.

CHAPTER NINE

WELL, it was too late for second thoughts now. First thing in the morning Sybilla was going to see Belinda and tell her that she intended to leave the business . . . to leave the area . . . but she still had the rest of today stretching out ahead of her . . . empty time to fill . . . and what better way to fill it than to go for a long walk, to stretch her legs and get some fresh air, and maybe some mental inspiration as to what she was going to do with the rest of her life?

The town was wreathed with footpaths and walks, and Sybilla chose one of the longer ones that followed the riverbank before ultimately climbing into the hills and from there joining one of the famous old drovers' roads.

Not that she intended to traverse the country or even the county—a few miles would be her limit and then home again.

She had gone less than three miles when her heel started to rub and she realised that she was getting a blister. She was close enough to the town to take a short-cut across a field and through the civic park, even though she was limping by the time she reached the chemist.

He was sympathetic while she explained her plight, suggesting that she use the ancient Windsor chair he always kept handy for some of his more elderly customers to sit in as she applied the plaster to her broken skin.

Thanking him, she did as he suggested and then put her sock back on and fastened her trainer. The trouble was that these were new trainers, and—despite their expensive price—rather more fashionable than comfortable.

She had bought them in a fit of extravagance which she was now regretting, and she certainly wasn't going to be able to walk any further in them, even with the comfort of the plaster between her sock and her chafed flesh, she acknowledged as she limped outside. Which meant that she would have to walk into the town square and catch a bus home.

The street was empty, and she was halfway down it when someone came up behind her, taking hold of her arm and pushing her back against the nearby wall.

As she tried to pull away in shock and panic she heard Ray Lewis's voice saying tauntingly, 'Well, now . . . not in too much of a rush to say hello to an old friend, are you?'

Although his words were innocuous enough, his manner wasn't, and nor was the way he was holding on to her, his fingers digging into her flesh as he forced her back against the wall, his body between her and anyone who might have passed by and recognised her plight, his body far, far too close to hers as he took first one and then another step closer to her, making her shrink back against the rough stone wall until she could feel its abrasive texture even through her thick sweater.

Her heart was beating frantically with fear, the fear that every woman knew under the threat of a man who felt no love for her, only lust and hatred.

'Not quite so full of yourself now, are you?' he was sneering at her, plainly enjoying her panic... her fear, even while she struggled to control them, to hide them from him. 'Think yourself so special, don't you? Well, I've got news for you. You're not special at all. You're just like all the rest. Now ask me nicely and I might just be persuaded to let you go.'

His free hand reached out to touch her face, but she flinched back from him, dodging his touch... her eyes as feral as a wildcat's, her whole body rejecting both his presence and his taunts.

'Going to play stubborn, are you? Well, I don't mind. The more stubborn you are, the more pleasure I'm going to get.'

'Sybilla, are you all right?'

The sound of Gareth's voice had never been more welcome. Almost instantly she was free, Ray Lewis muttering something about having an appointment to keep, almost running down the street as Gareth turned to her, demanding roughly, 'What the hell was going on?'

She was trembling so much that she could hardly speak. She saw the way Gareth frowned as he looked down the street after Ray Lewis, and instinctively she reached out, grabbing his arm with trembling fingers as she begged huskily, 'No, Gareth, please don't leave me.'

She was running on pure instinct, logic, caution; all the emotions she had taught herself to feel in place of the ones she would naturally feel were submerged by reaction to the shock of fear she had just experienced.

All she knew was that she didn't want Gareth to leave her... that she needed to be with him more than she had needed anything in her life, that even if his intent was to pursue Ray Lewis and punish him for what he had done to her she would still rather he stayed with her; she needed the comfort of his presence much more than she needed his vengeance against her aggressor.

She was trembling so hard that she knew he must feel it. He turned his head, his frown deepening as he studied her.

He lifted his hand to her face, touching it gently. 'If he hurt you . . .'

She shook her head, too emotionally vulnerable to risk speech. Someone else was walking past and Gareth stepped sideways to make room for them, inadvertently pulling her with him. When he heard her sharp gasp of pain and saw that she was limping he demanded curtly, 'What the hell——?'

'A blister. I blistered my heel. It's these new trainers...' She was babbling... her voice unnaturally high and strained. 'I was going to get the bus, that's when...' She wanted to stop, to dam the incessant stream of too high, too revealing words, but they refused to be dammed.

'The bus? Don't be ridiculous! I'll run you home. My car's parked in the square. Can you walk that far or would you prefer to stay here while I get it?'

Immediately she clutched harder at the arm she was holding, unaware that she was digging her nails into his flesh in her panic.

'No...no, Gareth...please...I can walk.'

But when she actually tried all she could manage were a few faltering steps before a combination of shock and pain made her stumble.

'Right, that's it,' Gareth told her tautly, and before she could stop him he turned towards her and picked her up, swinging her into his arms as though she weighed no more than a child.

'Gareth,' she protested frantically, 'people will see.'

Her eyes were almost on a level with his. He stopped mid-pace and gave her a look she could almost have described as brooding as he demanded slowly, 'So what?'

What could she say? She swallowed nervously and tried to concentrate on the throbbing pain in her heel; on the fear she had experienced when Ray Lewis had caught hold of her; on anything but the sensation of being in Gareth's arms...of being held close to his body, of feeling his heartbeat, which, despite the fact that he claimed that she wasn't too heavy, was so fast and so loud that she was terrified he might over-strain himself.

'I can walk the rest of the way,' she told him as they reached the square. 'Where is your car?'

'On the other side,' he told her grimly, 'and you aren't doing any walking.'

She didn't want to argue with him and put even more of a strain on his energy, and so instead she tried to concentrate on making herself as still as possible and of course on ignoring the pleasure her body was deriving from its contact with his, from the sensation of his arms around it, holding it... protecting it... arousing it.

Stop it, she warned herself, only able to release her breath when they reached his car and he put her down.

He still kept one arm around her, though, even when he stopped to unlock the passenger-door for her.

As he tucked her gently, tenderly almost, into the car his manner towards her was in direct contrast to the cold anger in his voice as he told her, 'I think it's time I had a word with Lewis.'

Sybilla shuddered, unable to stop herself, causing him to go very still and demand huskily, 'Are you sure he didn't hurt you...threaten you?'

Sybilla shook her head. 'No. I'm fine. Please...just leave it, will you, Gareth? It won't happen again. Not now that I've decided to——'

She only just stopped herself in time. Another few seconds and, in her vulnerable and over-weak state, she would have told Gareth about her plans to leave.

'Not now that you've decided to what?' he asked her.

She shook her head. 'It's nothing. It's kind of you to offer me a lift, but I could have managed on the bus.'

'I've been trying to get in touch with you,' Gareth told her as he closed the door and then walked round to the driver's door, opening it.

Sybilla felt the car rock slightly as he slid into his seat and reached for the seatbelt. Despite the generous width of the seats, she was acutely conscious of how little room there was between them. As he adjusted his belt his shoulder touched hers. She stiffened immediately, shivering a little as she caught the fresh clean scent of his skin, the soap he used somehow subtly emphasising the musky

male warmth of him, so that she had a shockingly erotic and unwanted mental image of him
without his clothes, his body lean and male, alien
and exciting, arousing as he leaned towards her
in the shadowy half-light surrounding the bed on
which . . .

This time when she shuddered Gareth noticed,
demanding curtly, 'What's wrong? And don't tell
me "nothing". If Lewis—— '

'No. No, it's nothing. I'm just a little bit cold,'
she fibbed.

Why on earth had she ever allowed herself to
accept his offer of a lift? If she hadn't been so
panicked, so frightened by Ray Lewis she would
never have done so. Everything that she was feeling now . . . everything she was experiencing and
enduring was reinforcing her awareness of how
dangerous it would be for her to continue to live
here. She had to leave. She really had no option.

Lost in her own thoughts, it was only when she
saw the familiar line of cottages which ended in
her own coming into view and realised that
Gareth wasn't decreasing the speed that she
turned to him and said anxiously, 'Gareth, stop.
You're going past—— '

'I'm taking you back home with me,' he told
her calmly. When she started to protest, he
added, 'I've been trying to get in touch with you
all week . . .'

Her heart leapt, her whole body seized by a surge of delight and confusion until he added prosaically, 'You still haven't collected the Dresden, and besides, despite your protests, I think Lewis upset you rather more than you want to admit. You really ought to report him to the police, you know.'

'For what?' she asked wryly. 'Wanting to have an affair with me?' She shook her head, and then realised in angry consternation that while Gareth had been talking to her they had covered the distance between her home and his and that he was now turning into the familiar drive to the Cedars.

It was too late now to demand that he stop the car. She should have done that earlier.

'I'm sorry I haven't collected the china,' she apologised stiffly to him as he brought the car to a halt outside the house. 'I had meant to, but...' She gave a tiny shrug, unable to admit to him just why she hadn't felt able to come up to the house while she knew he was there.

'Gramps always intended you to have it,' Gareth told her. 'Hang on,' he added as he unclipped his own seatbelt. 'I'll carry you inside.'

'No, please,' Sybilla protested, quickly unclipping her own seatbelt and reaching for the door. 'I'm fine now, really. It was just...just the shock.'

'What about your foot?'

Her foot? She stared at him for a moment and then flushed wildly, realising what he meant. She had almost forgotten the discomfort of her blistered heel.

'Oh, that. Oh, it will be fine. The plaster should protect it.'

It did, but only partially; the constant earlier friction must have resulted in the skin on her heel swelling, so, despite the plaster, she was still aware of pressure from her new trainers rubbing painfully against her flesh as she limped towards the house.

Gareth unlocked the door, and as she stepped into the familiar parquet-floored hall it was a bit like stepping backwards in time.

Nothing had changed here: the same curtains still hung at the windows, the same polished oak table was still there, the same rugs, the same air of solid Victorian dependability and sturdiness.

The Cedars wasn't pretty, but it was a strong, well-built house; the kind of house that immediately made you feel secure . . . warm . . . safe.

'I'll put the kettle on,' Gareth suggested, but Sybilla stopped him, shaking her head as she said quickly, 'No, please. I've already taken up more than enough of your time, Gareth. I'll just collect the china and . . .'

'It's upstairs in Gramps's room,' he told her.

'Of course. I'd forgotten for the moment.'
Tom Seymour had had the old-fashioned china
display cupboard moved upstairs into his bedroom because, as he had once told Sybilla, when
he couldn't sleep at night he liked to lie in bed and
imagine that the delicate china figures were about
to come to life, to go about their bucolic pur-
suits.

She knew the way as well as she knew the way
up her own stairs, but a certain diffidence made
her hesitate and glance enquiringly at Gareth before she turned towards them.

'Not forgotten the way, have you?'

A sudden constraint seemed to be oppressing
them both, as though for some reason Gareth too
was reluctant to move towards the stairs.

What on earth did he think she was going to
do, she wondered bitterly—pounce on him and
have her evil way with him?

'If you're worried about going into Gramps's
room...'

The quiet, almost hesitant words shamed her.
She felt tears of guilt sting her eyes and she shook
her head, unable to look at him as she told him
huskily, 'No. I...I saw your grandfather the
evening before he died. He seemed so well...so
relaxed...and that's how I'll always remember
him. And he was happy, Gareth,' she added,
taking an impulsive step towards him, suddenly
wanting to reassure him that, while the shock of

his grandfather's fatal heart attack had been traumatic for those who loved him, Tom Seymour himself had enjoyed his life right up until its end.

'Yes, I know. I spoke to him on the phone myself only hours before... before he died. If he had any awareness, any premonition of what was to happen, he certainly didn't betray it to me, but that doesn't lessen the sense of guilt, the sense of failure... the belief that I should have been here with him.'

'I know what you mean,' Sybilla told him in a low voice, admitting, 'I felt the same thing. I used to call round most evenings, but on that particular evening I'd been to a meeting of the Chamber of Commerce that ran particularly late. I've often thought since that if only I had come round as normal...'

'It wouldn't have made any difference,' Gareth assured her. 'The attack came in the early hours of the morning, and was so severe that he probably died without even waking up, the doctor told me. I still miss him, you know,' he added, his admission surprising her a little. 'Oh, I know I didn't see much of him... didn't come home as often as perhaps I should have, but he understood... and——' He stopped abruptly, and said almost roughly to her, 'Heaven knows why I'm burdening you with all this maudlin stuff. I'll come up and give you a hand with the china. I managed to find a box and some tissue-paper, and if I hadn't been able to get in touch with you this week I had intended to pack it all up and bring it round to your place and leave it in your garage.'

She wanted to ask him why he hadn't done that anyway, but the brief shared moment of intimacy and memory was over, and he was as distant from her as he had been ever since the morning she had discovered how much he resented her childish adoration and the burdens it placed on him.

She wanted to tell him that she could manage on her own, but it was, after all, his house and not hers, even though once she had run in and out of these rooms as though they were indeed her home.

As she walked up the stairs emotional tears blurred her eyes a little, making the traditional pattern on the red carpet waver. The curved wood of the banister rail felt smooth and warm beneath her fingertips, the light flooding in through the window halfway up the stairs where there was a small half-landing.

The house wasn't overly large for a house of its age: six very large bedrooms, and three smaller ones which had all now been converted into extra bathrooms, an attic floor where she had roamed happily as a child, and four large square comfortable rooms downstairs in addition to the kitchen and pantries.

All in all a very good-sized family home, and one where she was sure Gareth's wife and children would enjoy living when he ... She stopped on the stairs, her body caught in the vice-like grip of a pain so intense that she couldn't move.

Behind her she heard Gareth say her name, freeing her from the paralysis of her pain, enabling her somehow to move groggily upwards.

At the top of the stairs he caught up with her, placing his hands on her shoulders. Another moment and he would have turned her round and would be able to see the grief ... the pain ... the torment ... she was trying so hard to hide from him.

'Look, if this is too much for you ...'

He knew. The breath seized in her lungs as wild panic flooded through her. She started to turn towards him and then heard him saying, 'I know how much you loved Gramps, Syb.'

The panic subsided. She was able to step away from him and turn towards Tom's bedroom.

He had thought it was her love for his grandfather, her memories of him that were affecting her so emotionally, when in reality ...

He moved ahead of her, opening the door, ushering her inside, watching her anxiously.

Everything in the room was as it had always been, none of the furniture had been moved, but

Tom's familiar articles of clothing...his hair-brushes, his old dressing-gown...these were gone, so it was just a room, furnished with heavy old-fashioned furniture, with a double silver-framed photograph of a tense-looking and very young couple posed in their wedding finery standing on top of one of the oak chests, and against one wall, where it could be seen clearly from the bed, was the china cabinet.

Sybilla walked towards it slowly, her whole body trembling as she kneeled on the floor and turned the small key in the locked glass doors of the cabinet.

Inside, the delicate pastel colours of the Dresden figures blurred as her eyes filled with tears. They were a valuable as well as an emotional bequest...something she would treasure for all of her life.

Behind her she heard Gareth saying huskily, 'He always used to say that the shepherdesses reminded him of you...that you possessed the same delicate fragility...the same delicacy of complexion. He loved you very dearly...'

'As I did him.'

'I know.'

'Look, let me go downstairs and make that cup of tea. We both need it, and then we'll tackle this lot.'

Sybilla was about to shake her head and refuse when the phone rang downstairs.

'I'd better go down and answer that. That was one thing Gramps always refused to do, wasn't it? To have an extension installed upstairs.'

The telephone was in the hall, and with the bedroom door open, even though she wasn't deliberately eavesdropping, Sybilla soon realised that the call was from the factory and, from the sound of it, it was going to last for quite some time.

She stared at the Dresden figurines and reached into the cabinet to pick up one of them. Her hands were shaking as she wrapped it in tissue-paper. She mustn't break it...mustn't damage it. She hadn't realised how very emotional coming into the house was going to make her, partially because of her memories of Gareth and partially because of Tom himself, whom she did very sorely miss.

They had been good friends, despite the age gap between them. She had loved him and he had loved her, and she suspected that he had perhaps always known exactly why she had deliberately avoided being in town whenever Gareth was due home.

As she stood up she realised how dark it had gone outside, the wind whipping up black storm-clouds of rain.

Without intending it to happen, she wandered out on to the landing. A shared bathroom separated Tom's room from the room which had always been Gareth's.

How often as a child had she come bounding up the stairs, knocking briefly on Gareth's door before flinging it open and rushing inside! It had once been as familiar to her as her own bedroom at home.

She hesitated for a moment on the landing. Downstairs, Gareth was still speaking into the telephone receiver. Slowly she walked towards his bedroom door. It was already half open; all she had to do was give it a small push and then walk inside.

Nothing had changed; the familiar battered posters still adorned one wall, not of pin-up girls, but of huge blown-up photographs of various star systems, reminding her of Gareth's late-teenage fascination with the night sky. She smiled reminiscently as she looked at them, remembering the very first time her mother had allowed her to stay up late enough for Gareth to show her her first lunar eclipse. She had fallen asleep on his bed afterwards... he had woken her up with cocoa and biscuits.

She looked at the bed now and, as though drawn by a magnet, walked unsteadily over to it.

Gone was the teenage duvet with the Harley Davidson motorbike pictured on it, and in its place a set of crisp white linen.

If she touched it the linen would feel heavy and old. It had originally been a wedding present to his great grandmother, and Mrs Cooke, who had been Tom's daily for years, used to complain that it was the devil's work starching and ironing it. When she'd retired, and a new daily had had to be found, Tom had been persuaded to send the linen to a local laundry.

Every item was embroidered with the bride's initials. Who these days prepared for marriage like that? No one bought linen that would last through several lifetimes these days. Why bother, when often the marriage itself didn't last much longer than it took for the bright colours of modern manmade fabrics to grow dull and faded?

Telling herself she was being unfairly cynical, she tried not to look at the bed, tried not to imagine Gareth's dark head against the whiteness of the pillows, his skin tanned...silky... warm to the touch.

She discovered that she was actually stroking her fingers against the linen, smoothing it as though she were actually stroking Gareth's skin.

She snatched her hand away, trembling with shock and guilt, as she heard Gareth saying her name quietly.

When she swung round she saw that he had closed the door and was leaning against it, an odd expression in his eyes.

Over-burdened by guilt and emotional strain, she reacted instinctively, ignoring the fact that there was no way she could get through the closed door with him leaning against it and almost stumbling in her frantic haste to escape, her fingers trembling as she tried to grab hold of the door-handle and instead discovered that she was being held between Gareth's hands, his fingers biting into the bones of her shoulders.

He was angry with her because he had found her in his room, invading his privacy, she thought in confusion. If she apologised... explained he would let her go and then she would be safe. Once he had stopped touching her everything would be all right... everything would go back to normal... she would be safe.

'Gareth, p-please,' she started to stammer, but he cut ruthlessly through her intended apology, stunning her with the raw emotion in his voice as he mimicked,

'Gareth, please... what? Gareth, please kiss me... Gareth, please touch me... Gareth, please love me?'

She felt sick with shame... with humiliation, with a hundred and one other painful negative emotions, but even as she tried to pull away from him, instinctively trying to conceal her vulnerability from him, he pulled her hard against his body, his hands sliding down over her back, locking in the small of her back as he swung her round, imprisoning her against the door with the weight and bulk of his body, even while his hands protected her, cushioned her from any painful contact with the hardwood.

As she raised her head to plead with him, to beg him to cease this torment and let her go, he lowered his own.

The realisation that he was going to kiss her came too late for her to take evasive action. Her mouth softened ... opened slightly on a breathless gasp of disbelief.

She felt the hard demanding pressure of his mouth against her own; her brain almost stupefied by the belated realisation that this was a kiss of intense passion, of intense desire, a kiss of the kind of intimacy shared only by established acknowledged lovers, a kiss that couldn't be refused or rejected even if she had been able to do so, even if she had been physically able to stop her lips clinging to his mouth, to stop them opening, softening, swelling eagerly as they returned the intimacy he was offering them, the intimacy to explore the outline of his mouth with her tongue-tip, to stroke its moistness, to tug wantonly on the fullness of his bottom lip with the tender sharpness of her teeth and to submit in shivering excitement and arousal to the deep thrust of his tongue within her mouth, while his hands caressed her back all the way down to the soft curves of her buttocks in time with the slow

building rhythmic penetration of his tongue
within the receptive moistness of her mouth.

It was a dream; totally unreal; totally impossible; a fantasy beyond even her wildest imaginings, impossible to resist or reject.

When Sybilla found the strength to open her
dazed, desire-drugged eyes Gareth was looking
back at her.

Why had she never realised that grey eyes could
look so hot, that desire could make their coolness smoulder and burn so that she almost
flinched beneath that heat?

His mouth left hers and she ached from its loss,
unconsciously sighing and focusing on it, touching her bereft lips with the tip of her tongue, so
unaware of what she was betraying that the shock
of his reaction to it, as he groaned and pushed her
back against the door, his hands framing her
face, holding her head still, made it impossible
for her to do anything to control the wild jolt of
sensation racking her body when his mouth covered hers for a second time.

Her hands found his back, at first clinging to
him for support, and then relaxing, stroking, caressing, exploring, unconsciously mimicking the
deepening passion of his kiss as she moved
against him, wanting him ... needing him ...
loving him.

She tugged his shirt free of his belt, shivering
with pleasure as she touched his bare skin, trac-

ing the bones of his spine, measuring the width of
his shoulders, sliding her open palms over his
skin, absorbing its heat, its strength, its satin
texture, while her body ached to know him with
every one of her other senses as well...his
scent...his taste...his husky male sounds of need
and pleasure; she craved the knowledge, the intimacy of these as much as she craved his hands
against her body, his flesh within her own.

And even when she heard herself telling him
so, whispering the ragged words between kisses
which were escalating so fast to such a hitherto
unknown degree of intimacy that she was already lost, gone far, far beyond the recall of her
frantic brain's pleas for caution, she couldn't stop
herself.

'This; you want this?' she heard Gareth demanding rawly as he slid his hands beneath her
jumper, spanning her ribcage, stroking lightly
against the fine silk that enclosed her breasts, her
skin so sensitive, her need so acute that just that
lightest brushing of his fingertips against it was
enough to make her cry out softly, her body
shivering with sexual tension, her breasts already
swollen, aching.

'Gareth...please.'

'What is it? What is it you want? Is it this?'

His thumbs moved softly against her nipples,
making her whimper frantically and arch against

him and then cry out in frustration when he stopped touching her.

'Shush. It's all right . . . it's all right.'

The soothing words were whispered against her ear, but her body was too feverishly aroused to heed them, so he groaned out loud as she continued to twist and turn frantically against him, blindly seeking relief of the ache burning her flesh, hindering him in his attempts to remove her sweater.

It was only when she felt the shaft of cool air touch her skin that she realised what he was doing, her body stilling as she waited breathlessly for him to relieve her of its burden.

'Beautiful, you're so beautiful. I always knew you'd be just like this.'

The words were whispered against her skin like silk, hot moist silk, just like the slow kisses burning her collarbone, her throat.

She tugged frantically at the front of his shirt, wanting to caress him as he was doing her, wanting to bury her hot mouth in the cool enticement of his skin, to lap at his flesh with eager, delicate, cat-like licks so that he cried out beneath its delicate abrasion, wanting her with the same intensity with which she wanted him.

She had no awareness of how she had come by this new sensual knowledge, this awareness of the erotic complicity and allure of touch and taste, of need and desire; she only knew that she wanted his body open and receptive to the exploration of her hands and her mouth just as much as her own flesh ached for that same intimacy and desire from him.

When he stopped kissing her she couldn't bear the loss of physical contact, sliding her hands into his hair, holding him against her body, willing him to feel the need that burned inside her, making her breasts softly swollen, her nipples tight and hard.

She almost sobbed in relief as she felt the heat of his breath between her breasts, the caress of his mouth as it slid over her skin.

She had forgotten that she was still wearing her bra, but she couldn't endure it if he stopped what he was doing now, and somehow or other he seemed to realise it because his mouth slid over the curve of her breasts, over the silk; over the taut peak of her nipple where it settled and then suckled, slowly at first, hesitantly almost, as though he was afraid to hurt her, and then, when he recognised the need behind the stifled whimpers of pleasure emerging from her throat, he was less gentle, much less gentle, rough almost, as if he was sharing the same rip-tide of desire which had engulfed her.

Without the pressure of his body to hold her upright against the door, she suspected she would probably have collapsed, her body had become so weak, so sensually obsessed with his.

When his teeth raked her nipple she cried out in pleasure, arching her back, curling her fingers into his hair, repeating his name over and over again in a rhythmic litany that unconsciously echoed the rising pulse of her own arousal.

When Gareth leaned against her she melted inside, returning the pressure of his body as he slowly stood up. The silk of her bra clung moistly to her breast where he had suckled on it, outlining the tautness of her nipple. Gareth brushed his thumb slowly over it and then repeated the caress a little more roughly so that the friction of the damp fabric against her tender skin made her ache for the warm abrasion of his lips...his tongue...his teeth.

She started to shiver, and instantly he stopped, apologising rawly, 'I'm sorry. It's just that you...God, Syb, you're turning me inside out, do you know that? I want you so much that I could take you here and now where we're standing, and then still go on wanting you so that by the time I'd carried you to my bed I'd want you all over again, but the last thing I want to do is hurt you,' he told her broodingly.

His words should have shocked her back to reality, but instead they added dangerously volatile fuel to the fire already raging inside her, bringing to life needs that whispered so shockingly, so wantonly to her that it was impossible to resist their enticement.

Against his ear she told him shakily and huskily, 'You weren't hurting me, and . . . and I didn't want you to stop.'

She shuddered again, unable to control what she was feeling, and forced herself to look at him while she did so, knowing what he must read in her eyes.

'This . . . you want this again?' he demanded with rough, almost disbelieving pleasure, his thumb slowly caressing her.

'Yes. Yes. But . . . but this time without anything between us,' she implored him; and then as he complied, quickly unsnapping her bra so that she could let it fall away from her body, and she felt the fierce spirals of reaction beginning to tighten inside her, she managed to tell him huskily, 'And your mouth, Gareth. Please, I want your mouth as well.'

She thought she heard him groan, but she might have been mistaken. However, she knew that he had heard her as seconds later she was shuddering with quickening delight as his mouth tugged fiercely on her eager flesh.

She didn't know when he unzipped her jeans. Didn't know how he managed to ease her out of them without her registering it, that awareness completely submerged by the fierce paroxysm of pleasure that gripped her as his hand slid between her legs, caressed her body, while he whispered lavish words of praise into her ear, telling her how much he ached for closer contact with its soft moistness, how much pleasure it gave him to caress her so intimately.

Sybilla heard him, but couldn't make any verbal response to him as her body reacted to his touch.

Her hands moved up under his shirt and down over his back, registering its damp slickness as she tried to close the distance between them and to satisfy the ache pulsing deep inside her with a more intimate contact with him, but he stopped her, kissing her quickly and then telling her huskily, 'No, Syb. I can't . . . I daren't . . . I . . .'

She couldn't bear it . . . couldn't endure it. She would die if he didn't ease the ache within her now in the only way every instinct she possessed told her it could be eased.

Pride, self-respect, caution were all forgotten as she pressed herself against him, rotating her hips, pleading openly, 'Gareth . . . please . . . please don't say that . . . Not now. I need you so much. I . . .'

She hadn't realised she was actually crying until he cupped her face, groaning as he licked away her tears.

'And don't you think it's exactly the same for me? That I want you just as much? For God's sake, Syb. Feel . . . feel what you're doing to me.'

When he took her hand and placed it against his body he shuddered, his flesh so taut . . . so hard beneath her fingers that she automatically made a tiny mewing sound of distress deep in her throat and pleaded, 'Gareth, please ... please now. I want you now ... now ... now ...'

She was no longer in control of what she was saying ... what she was doing ... what she was inviting; a deeper, age-old instinct had taken over from reality and logic, an instinct that possessed her ... drove her ... making her say and do things that would normally have made her blench with horror and disbelief.

She felt Gareth move, levering himself away from her, and she reached out towards him despairingly, clutching at his shirt, closing her eyes so that she wouldn't have to watch him walk away from her.

'Shush ... it's all right ... it's all right,' he told her roughly, and suddenly, blissfully, unbelievably it was.

He had removed his jeans, removed everything bar the shirt from which she had virtually ripped all the buttons in her attempts to get closer to his body, and now he was removing the rest of her clothes as well, pausing briefly to lightly suckle both breasts before picking her up.

As she wrapped her body around his she felt him shudder, his teeth biting sharply into her throat as he protested rawly, 'Syb, please. It's my first time with you and I want to make it last forever, but, with what you're doing to me right now, I don't think I can even make it over to the bed.'

For some reason the words excited her, aroused her, inciting her to a wantonness she would have sworn was completely alien to her nature, so that she moved eagerly against him and urged him, 'Now, Gareth. I want you now . . . please now.'

The result was inevitable, the sensation of being pushed back against the door, while Gareth cushioned her back from the impact as best he could, so erotically satisfying that her whole body seemed to melt against him, welcoming the surging power of him, her legs tightening around him, locking him against her as he started to kiss her, his tongue mirroring the penetrating strength of his body.

He was her first lover, and yet her body welcomed him as though it had known him forever, clinging silkily to him, closing lovingly around him, welcoming him, cherishing him so that the pleasure she was giving him was repaid in full as her body reacted to the delight of knowing him so intimately, tiny coiling spirals of pleasure beginning to build up inside her, making her cry out and cling, making her plead and praise, twist and ache, making her so totally uninhibited and giving that it was all he could do to control his own desire until he felt the first sharp contractions that marked her own climax.

When she cried out in shocked discovery, unable to stop herself from submitting to its domination, her eyes opened wide and she discovered that Gareth was looking right back at her and that it was too late now to conceal from him what she was feeling. It was like a clouded sky suddenly being rent apart by lightning, and she felt as overawed, as shocked and afraid almost as some long-ago primitive man might have felt at seeing the skies part to reveal a glimpse of immortality. And then, just when she thought that it was over, that she had scaled the highest mortal peak, she trembled under the sensation of being filled with the pulsing heat of Gareth's own completion, her body so sensitive to him that that pulsing emission set off tiny after-shocks of pleasure to stimulate her nerve-endings.

'Gareth . . .'

'Shush,' he murmured as he kissed her and slowly shifted her weight in his arms. 'Not now. What I want now is to take you to bed, to hold you and to go on holding you.'

He was carrying her across to his bed, pushing back the covers, sliding her into its delicious coolness, easing his body down against hers, holding her. She ought not to be doing this, her brain warned her, but it was what her body craved, and her senses overruled the weak voice of her brain.

*   *   *

When Sybilla woke up later it was dark.

'Hungry?' Gareth asked her, somehow sensing that she was awake, even though she hadn't moved.

Uncertainly she shook her head, unable to believe what she had done...that she and Gareth...

'No, neither am I...at least, not for food,' he told her lazily. 'But when it comes to you, my love, I have an appetite that isn't going to be easily appeased at all.'

Still in shock, she felt him turn her towards him and start kissing her. She tried weakly not to respond, but her body seemed to have other ideas.

As he kissed her Gareth told her, 'I still can't believe this is really happening. After all this time. And to be your first lover.'

He felt her tense and said tenderly, 'Did you think I wouldn't know...or that I wouldn't care? Do you really think me so crass?' His finger traced the shape of her upper lip.

'This time it's going to be different,' he told her huskily. 'This time it's going to be so slow and gentle that it will feel as if the pleasure's going to last forever.'

It was all he had promised her and more: a slow, sweet build-up followed by an equally sweet, almost agonising release and then the delicious drift of his mouth over her skin, at first soothing it and then arousing it so that she actually cried out for the intimate invasion of his tongue within her body, welcoming the unexpected surge of quickening pleasure that overtook her and made her cling pleadingly to him, wantonly imploring him to let her caress him as intimately as he had done her.

Afterwards she slept as deeply as a child, while he watched her, wondering if she knew yet just how much she had betrayed to him and what she would do once she did.

Perhaps she thought that because no words of love had passed her lips he wouldn't know.

He touched her tenderly, sighing. He was equally at fault; he could have told her... should have told her, but he had wanted to hear it first from her... after all the years of yearning... wanting... aching for her.

She had given herself so generously to him— was he a fool to want her to give her love equally generously, equally freely?

The next time Sybilla woke up it was light. Gareth still slept beside her, bringing her a shocked return to reality, to the knowledge of what she had done... how she had behaved. Her face burned with embarrassment and confusion. How could she have? She shuddered, crawling quickly from the bed ... Gareth's bed.

Useless trying to deny the pleasure her body had found there... the pleasure it had given, but to have had that pleasure without an equal meas-

ure of love—that was what she could not understand...not in Gareth, who was, after all, a male
and alien in so many unfathomable and unknown ways, but in herself, whom she had
thought she had known inside-out.

She dressed quickly, not risking taking a
shower, and somehow guiltily enjoying the scent
of Gareth on her skin. Outside, the air was clear
and cold still, the sun hidden behind misty cloud.
She wandered aimlessly through the garden but
ended up, as she had known she must, not far
from the summer house where she had overhead
that fateful conversation between Gareth and his
grandfather. She sat down on a stone bench, her
chin cupped in her hands. She couldn't stay on in
town now. That was impossible. She doubted if
she could even bring herself to face Gareth.

What on earth would he think when he woke
up and remembered? The best thing for both of
them would be if they never had to see one another again. He would want to be confronted
with the reality of what had occurred between
them as little as she did herself.

She stared miserably at the weed choking the
small plant growing at her feet, tugging fiercely
at it, wincing as its sharp leaves tore her skin,
tears of pain and despair flooding her eyes.

'I thought I might find you here.'

She stiffened as she heard Gareth's voice behind her.

'This always used to be one of your favourite spots.' He paused and then told her gently, 'We need to talk, you and I, don't we?'

It was his gentleness that hurt the most, his determination not to shirk or avoid confronting what had happened when she knew with painful honesty that it had been *her* desire . . . *her* wantonness . . . *her* initiation more than his that had led to what had happened between them.

'Would it help if I go first?' he offered lightly.

For a moment she was almost tempted to smile, but she was too afraid for laughter . . . too raw inside emotionally . . . too aware of how badly she had behaved.

Without waiting for her reply, Gareth continued steadily, 'It was down here that I first realised two things of vital importance to my life. The first was that I love you . . . the second was that I had no right to burden you with that love since you were virtually still a child, while I . . . well, legally, at any rate, I was an adult. That I had somehow to separate myself from you and allow you to grow up unburdened by my needs . . . my emotions. You see, Sybilla, I knew how easy it would be to betray both you and myself by exploiting the adolescent emotions you were beginning to feel for me, and so I decided our friendship must end. Not without a good deal of heart-searching, I can tell you.

'And so when you started to distance yourself from me I told myself that I was glad...that it was only right that you should grow outwards towards boys of your own age and not inwards towards me, and yet I hated it...loathed it...was bitterly, searingly jealous...ached for you so much that I could have committed murder to have you.

'In the end it got too much for me to endure. I thought you must have guessed how I felt, you were so cold towards me. I decided to leave the country, to give you time to grow up and myself time to control what I felt for you. Later, when you were adult, there would be time for us to come together if that was what fate planned for us...to meet as two adults; and yet whenever I did come home you were very carefully not here, and the love I felt for you began to corrode inside me to make me bitter and angry.

'You didn't want me. You were never going to want me. From my grandfather I learned how well you were doing, how your life was filled with your career, your friends...the men who admired and wanted you. He knew how I felt...pitied me for it, I think...certainly tried to warn me not to hope for something you might never want to give me...and then he died, and I came back.

'And almost immediately all the jealous imaginings of the years we'd been apart became reality—first when I saw that shaving-cream and then when I saw you with Lewis. Your lover...or so I thought.

'I couldn't handle it...couldn't take it...I misjudged you, and I hurt you...but nothing like as much as I hurt myself.

'And then I found out that there wasn't anyone special in your life...that when I kissed you you melted in my arms and responded to me the way I'd always ached for you to do, but ''you knew how I felt'', you told me, and I thought you were rejecting my love, telling me that, while you acknowledged a certain degree of physical desire for me, you didn't love me.

'But you'd kept the pig...my pig...the one I'd won for you, and when it got broken you cried and you kept the pieces. I started hoping then...praying. Why didn't you tell me last night when we made love that you loved me? You told me everything else?'

She couldn't help it—she felt engulfing her skin a blush that began at her toes and spread all over her body.

'You can't mean any of this, Gareth,' she protested thickly. 'I know you *don't* love me. I overheard you years ago, complaining to your grandfather that my...my adolescent crush on you was a nuisance.'

She couldn't look at him ... couldn't do anything other than suffer in the suffocating silence that followed her outburst.

'You heard *that*?'

She nodded. 'Yes, that's why... that's why I started avoiding you. I couldn't bear it, knowing how much you despised me for what I felt... knowing how much of a child I must seem to you.'

'Oh, Sybilla, no. It wasn't like that. Oh, my darling, don't cry... not if you want me to tell you what that conversation was really about. I promise you, if you don't stop crying, I'm going to have to stop you by kissing you, and we both know what will happen then, don't we?'

When had he moved so close to her that as she turned to look at him he was able to take her in his arms and hold her so that she couldn't avoid looking at him?

'What you overheard was only *part* of a conversation. A conversation during which I'd admitted to my grandfather how I felt about you... during which I'd acknowledged that I was aware of your growing feelings for me and how afraid I was of exploiting them. He had been warning me against that temptation... that danger... and I trying to remove some of the emotion from our discussion, making light of what we were saying. My describing your crush as a nuisance was a shorthand message between my grandfather and myself that was just a massive understatement of the true state of affairs. The truth was that I was terrified that in your artless innocence you might offer me what I so desperately wanted, and that I might, God forgive, take it and destroy your future along with my own because, at fifteen, you were much, much too young to make the kind of commitment I wanted from you.'

'I can't believe I'm hearing this,' Sybilla told him in a wobbly voice.

He smiled tenderly at her.

'Didn't last night prove to you just how much I love you? If I didn't say the words it was only because I so desperately wanted to hear them from you first, but then, when I realised I wasn't going to do so...

'I'm sorry if I hurt you. If I'd known... realised...'

'Perhaps it's just as well you didn't,' Sybilla admitted. 'If I'd guessed then when I was fifteen...' She gave a tiny shrug and blushed again. 'Well, I can't deny that, illegal though it might have been, the emotional intensity of the moment could have resulted in physical intimacy, and you were right. I was too young...much too young.'

'And now?' he whispered to her.

'And now I think I'm old enough to know my own mind...my own emotions. I have to admit it was a shock when I realised that I love you.' She smiled as she saw the look in his eyes and then told him, 'I did tell you, as well. Last night, when you were asleep. I couldn't help myself. I was going to leave town...to go away somewhere and make a fresh start...perhaps that was why—at least partially why, anyway—I behaved so recklessly yesterday.'

'Mm. You were reckless, weren't you?' he teased her. Then he added more soberly, 'I'm afraid we're going to have to have a very quick, very quiet wedding, my love. I can't swear that you haven't already conceived my child, and while I don't give a damn who knows how much I wanted you and how impetuously, for the sake of your parents and our child I think it might be best if we used a bit of discretion.

'With Gramps's death... Well, let's just say that a quiet wedding shouldn't seem too out of place.'

'You really think I might already be pregnant?' Sybilla asked him breathlessly.

He laughed when he saw the expression on her face. 'Well, if you feel like that about it, we could always...'

A good many people in the town announced that they weren't in the least surprised to hear that Gareth Seymour and Sybilla were getting married. After all, they had known one another for years ... had grown up together virtually. It was a pity, of course, that Tom Seymour couldn't have been alive to witness the ceremony, but in the circumstances it was only natural that the pair should prefer a quick, quiet wedding.

After all, they both carried heavy responsibilities, his for the factory and hers for her business. They had no house to buy since they were going to live at the Cedars, and, if the few chosen guests who did attend the small wedding breakfast were surprised by the groom's choice of a gift for his bride, she certainly seemed to find no fault with it.

As one woman remarked in surprise to her companion, 'Good heavens ... a pot pig ... and when you think of that beautiful Dresden that Tom left her ...'

'Not one pig. There were two,' her son pointed out to her. 'There was a little one as well.'

'Where on earth did you find it? Them?' Sybilla asked her new husband later when they were alone, as she lovingly touched her wedding gift. 'It's exactly the same.'

'I had a team of detectives scouring every street-market in existence,' he told her mock teasingly. 'Like this little fellow as well, do you?' he asked, picking up the smaller of the two pigs. 'You never know—he could be the first of many.'

'Oh, could he? And what makes you think he is a he?' she challenged. 'He could be a she.'

'Girl . . . boy . . . I don't mind,' Gareth assured her as he bent over to kiss her, murmuring dulcetly against her mouth, 'Though I still think that Thomasina is a dreadful name to inflict on a little girl. And just because you promised Gramps——'

'I promised him my first child was going to be named after him,' Sybilla began.

'Mm . . . so did I. Do you suppose he knew . . . knows?'

'It would be nice to think so,' Sybilla agreed tenderly. 'Thomasina . . . perhaps we could make that her second name.'

She was still laughing when Gareth rolled her over on the bed and beneath him.

HARLEQUIN®

PRESENTS *plus*

Meet Helen Palmer. She knows that as *single* mother of
the bride, she's going to have to spend time with Zack
Neilson, *single* father of the groom. Trouble is, Zack's
the man responsible for her broken heart.

And then there's Charlie MacEnnaly. When it rains it
pours! Not only is she forced to accept the hospitality of
business tycoon Phil Atmor—her only neighbor on
Norman's Island—she's forced to bunk in with Sam,
Phil's pet pig.

Helen and Charlie are just two of the passionate women
you'll discover each month in Harlequin Presents Plus.
And if you think they're passionate, wait until you meet
Zack and Phil!

Watch for
MOTHER OF THE BRIDE by Carole Mortimer
Harlequin Presents Plus #1607

and

SUMMER STORMS by Emma Goldrick
Harlequin Presents Plus #1608

Harlequin Presents Plus
The best has just gotten better!

Available in December wherever
Harlequin Books are sold.

PPLUS7

Take 4 bestselling love stories FREE

Plus get a FREE surprise gift!

POSTCARDS FROM EUROPE

HARLEQUIN PRESENTS®

Hi!
Spending a year in Europe. You won't believe how great the men are! Will be visiting Greece, Italy, France and more.
Wish you were here—how about joining us in January?

There's a handsome Greek just waiting to meet you.

THE ALPHA MAN
by Kay Thorpe

Harlequin Presents #1619

Available in January wherever Harlequin books are sold.

HPPFEG

When the only time you have for yourself is...

STOLEN *moments*™

Christmas is such a busy time—with shopping, decorating, writing cards, trimming trees, wrapping gifts....

When you do have a few *stolen moments* to call your own, treat yourself to a brand-new *short* novel. Relax with one of our Stocking Stuffers— or with all six!

Each STOLEN MOMENTS title is a complete and original contemporary romance that's the perfect length for the busy woman of the nineties! Especially at Christmas...

And they make perfect **stocking stuffers**, too! (For your mother, grandmother, daughters, friends, co-workers, neighbors, aunts, cousins—all the other women in your life!)

Look for the STOLEN MOMENTS display in December

STOCKING STUFFERS:

HIS MISTRESS Carrie Alexander
DANIEL'S DECEPTION Marie DeWitt
SNOW ANGEL Isolde Evans
THE FAMILY MAN Danielle Kelly
THE LONE WOLF Ellen Rogers
MONTANA CHRISTMAS Lynn Russell

HSM2

 **WORLDWIDE LIBRARY**

1993 Keepsake

Stories

Capture the spirit and romance of Christmas with KEEPSAKE CHRISTMAS STORIES, a collection of three stories by favorite historical authors. The perfect Christmas gift!

Don't miss these heartwarming stories, available in November wherever Harlequin books are sold:

ONCE UPON A CHRISTMAS by Curtiss Ann Matlock
A FAIRYTALE SEASON by Marianne Willman
TIDINGS OF JOY by Victoria Pade

**ADD A TOUCH OF ROMANCE TO YOUR
HOLIDAY SEASON WITH KEEPSAKE
CHRISTMAS STORIES!**

HX93

**Fifty red-blooded, white-hot, true-blue hunks
from every State in the Union!**

Look for MEN MADE IN AMERICA! Written by some
of our most poplar authors, these stories feature fifty of
the strongest, sexiest men, each from a different state in
the union!

Two titles available every other month at your favorite
retail outlet.

In November, look for:

STRAIGHT FROM THE HEART by Barbara Delinsky
(Connecticut)
AUTHOR'S CHOICE by Elizabeth August (Delaware)

In January, look for:

DREAM COME TRUE by Ann Major (Florida)
WAY OF THE WILLOW by Linda Shaw (Georgia)

You won't be able to resist MEN MADE IN AMERICA!